SOUTHERN GOTHIC SHORTS

NEW SHORT STORIES FROM THE WINNERS OF THE INAUGURAL
SOUTHERN GOTHIC SHORTS WRITING COMPETITION

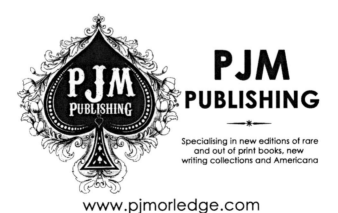

PJM
PUBLISHING

Specialising in new editions of rare
and out of print books, new
writing collections and Americana

www.pjmorledge.com

SOUTHERN GOTHIC SHORTS

NEW SHORT STORIES FROM THE WINNERS OF THE INAUGURAL
SOUTHERN GOTHIC SHORTS WRITING COMPETITION

COLLECTED BY

PHILLIP J. MORLEDGE

PJM
PUBLISHING

SOUTHERN GOTHIC SHORTS

© Copyright Phillip J. Morledge 2008

COVER PHOTOGRAPH - FOG IN THE FOREST BY DOUG BOWMAN

BACK COVER PHOTOGRAPH - PALMER CEMETARY FRIDAY 13TH BY ALANNA RALPH

COURTESY OF CREATIVE COMMONS SEARCH AND FLICKR

NEW EDITION PAPERBACK 2009

This Edition First Published JANUARY 2009

PJM Publishing Sheffield, England

ISBN 978-0-9559765-5-1

Contents

INTRODUCTION

'She felt the snake between her breasts, felt him there, and loved him there, coiled, the deep tumescent S held rigid, ready to strike. She loved the way the snake looked sewn onto her V-neck letter sweater, his hard diamondback pattern shining in the sun. It was unseasonably hot, almost sixty degrees, for early November in Mystic, Georgia, and she could smell the light musk of her own sweat.'

So began my introduction to that particular genre of American fiction known as Southern Gothic.

I chanced upon my tatty old copy of 'A Feast of Snakes' by Harry Crews in a charity shop I forget the name of. How it got there remains a mystery, but I like to think it was some dark providence at work, A paper doorway into another world I have been happy to inhabit ever since.

'Southern Gothic Shorts' brings together for the first time a collection of short stories each written in the

Southern Gothic style, a style that Francis Russell Hart described as 'fiction evocative of a sublime and picturesque landscape... depicting a world in ruins." New writers telling tales of the South and its inhabitants, its dark heart and redemptive skies. Tales of lost highways, flea bitten motels and the grotesque underbelly of small town life.

But for all that, what really stands out in this collection is the wide variety of styles and subject matter that can fall under the umbrella of the Southern Gothic genre. From heart warming tales of family and friendship to stories that almost literally drip with a sense of impending menace. What all the stories have in common, however, is a strong sense of place. Of a South moulded by its own history and sealed within its own geography, a South of the imagination as much as one grounded in the real.

I came across the Southern Gothic genre purely by chance, but since then my library has expanded and grown, with classics from the past and a whole host of current authors. Thankfully the passion for dark tales of the South is alive and well not just in the devoted reader but in the pens and imaginations of a whole new generation of writers. The stories collected here are just a small cross section of the wealth of talent that is out there. Hopefully it will serve as an introduction to some, a staging post for others, and most of all an inspiration for many more narratives to come.

PHILLIP J. MORLEDGE

SHEFFIELD DECEMBER 2008

The Pearl
by Kerry Donoghue

Harlan savored every burning drop of his gin as Jezebel drifted into the muddy Tennessee. The mosquitoes swarmed. He slapped one dead on his neck and enjoyed the slow afternoon buzz. The sun pulsed down like a dying heartbeat through the wilted dogwoods, the sweat beading across his upper lip, dripping down his temples. Harlan stretched his long legs and felt the perspiration river along the backs of his thighs, through the tangles of leg hair, into the dark valleys of his jean shorts. It was only noon and the heat was just getting started. After another sip, Harlan ate his sandwich and from the weedy riverbanks, watched his sister with his good eye.

Jezebel adjusted her snorkel mask and set her lips against the breathing tube. The sludge suctioned around her feet, each slogging step a cadence that lulled Harlan closer to sleep. She swam farther out, a plastic grocery bag trailing in her hand, billowing into the ripples. She dove under.

Harlan took a long swill until she surfaced. Jezebel beamed, waving something she'd found. He wanted to wave back to her, to let her know he saw and was proud, but it was too hot to lift his arm. It was too hot to do anything. He didn't want to move, not even to strip off his tank top and ball it like a pillow under his damp head. Harlan didn't know how she did it every day. What exactly was she hoping to find out there? She dove under again.

Damn girl's gonna drown. Harlan closed his eyes.

"You done yet, Harlan?"

Harlan twisted out of sleep to see his neighbor Mason squinting down at him.

"You fix the machine?"

Drool crackled off Harlan's chin as he yawned, tiny strands hardened like old garage cobwebs. Over the river, the sun was setting. He jerked awake. "Where's Jezebel?"

"Up at the house," Mason said.

"Thank God." The adrenaline pumping through him eddied into a throbbing headache.

"God got nothing to do with it. Jezebel's just three years younger than you and she's a fine swimmer."

"You sayin' I can't worry about my baby sister?"

"She's twenty-seven, Harlan. Ain't nothing baby 'bout that." He kicked the paper bag at Harlan's feet. An empty gin bottle edged out. "Didn't finish what I paid you for, I gather."

The world spun. Harlan anchored his feet and leaned his right hand on the ground. He shut his eyes, but it was worse that way so he focused on a rock. "Your washing machine'll be ready in the morning."

"If you weren't so damn good, I'd punch you, Harlan."

"That's what all the ladies say."

Mason sighed. "I'll come by at eight. Be ready."

Harlan tried to steady his hands to make the okay sign.

"Go help your sister," Mason said, shaking his head. He ambled down the banks back to his house.

Harlan rubbed his good eye as dusk tugged down the night. Hangovers were hard enough, but having only one sure eye made them even worse. Harlan was nine when one of Mama's manfriends clocked him across the cheek so hard that he knocked the sight clear out of him. He knew Mama was sorry because she'd let him eat chocolate chip pancakes for a full week afterwards. Besides, she'd made Harlan promise he'd never do that to a woman, and he'd held true to that his whole life. It was all just water under his never-ending bridge.

When he entered the house he shared with his sister and her two Catahoula hounds, Jezebel was crouched at the oven, prodding what smelled to be tuna casserole. "Back from the dead!" She laughed. "My cooking smell that good, Harlan? Or you out of gin?"

"I was just nappin', Jezz."

"Right, and tonight's a crawdad feast for supper." She pulled the casserole out of the oven while her hounds sniffed around her. "No matter. Pull up a seat." She scooped two servings in a dog dish for the hounds. They licked the food away in less than a minute before their gray and white speckled faces looked up at her again. "What else can I do for you, huh?" She grinned and gave them both another scoop.

"Come on, Jezz, I'm hungry." He stole a forkful from the dish.

Jezebel slapped his hand away. "Could you do it proper for once?" She heaped a steaming serving onto his paper plate. "Don't need another dog in this house."

Harlan eyed the hounds and wondered how many similarities there were between him and them. He decided not to ask her about that. "You find anything good out there today?"

She nodded towards a digital watch on the counter. "I found that, all tangled up in mud and roots. But I dove deep down and got it." She pointed the spoon at him and a glob of casserole fell off. "I'm gonna be just as good as all them Australian divers, you wait."

Jezebel practiced diving every day before her job as a polisher at the town jewelry store. She and her hounds rose with the sun and walked to the shore where she'd strip down and prepare to drag the river bottom. She could hold her breath for one minute and thirty-five seconds, although traditional Japanese divers could hold theirs for two full minutes. She'd read all about it in the photo book she'd borrowed from the library and couldn't bear to return.

"I can hold so much, Harlan. It's really happening."

Harlan considered Jezebel's petite frame and wide smile. Her forearms and calves were toned from swimming, something their mother had taught Jezebel in first grade, when the fights with Mama's friends started. Anytime one of Mama's men pounded the door or shattered a plate, Jezebel would run down to the river since it was right in their backyard and inch on in. Mama would run after her and yank her out until finally she said, "Well, you might as well learn how to get out if you get in." And she towed Jezebel out to where she couldn't stand and taught her how to swim. That was right before she made Harlan start babysitting Jezebel at night, which meant they stayed up late watching *Three's Company* re-runs and eating cinnamon sugar toast for dinner. Mama wouldn't get home until breakfast, but she always smelled like nighttime, an old sigh of gardenia and stale breath. It stayed that way until Mama died, a cracked vodka bottle at her feet and a pink smile smeared on her face.

Harlan saw it himself when he went to the morgue to identify her. He didn't tell Jezebel she was dead until after he made an eight-drink stop at his favorite bar.

Harlan blinked. With her blonde hair parted down the middle and gathered by a Chip Clip, Jezebel looked just like their mother. Standing at the stove, in their dead mother's house, a hand on her hip, she was their mother. But Mama had been cold for almost a year now. Harlan shook his head to clear it, touching the brown curls he got from their daddy. They hadn't seen him in years so Harlan didn't know what he'd end up looking like and that scared him if he thought about it too much.

They took their plates to the kitchen table like they'd done since they were little, sitting in fold-up seats at the heads of the table. A small television rested on a stack of cookbooks.

"Something good comin' up?" he asked between bites. The table wobbled. Or maybe he did. He sat up straighter.

"Always. It's seven-thirty, Harlan." Jezebel turned the volume knob until she heard the familiar voice reel, "Wheel of Fortune!" She clapped and then scooted back to her chair, her eyes locked on the television.

"What you waitin' for, Jezebel?" He scraped his plate.

"For this," she whispered. "Stop ruining it for me."

Vanna White floated onto the screen in a royal blue sequined gown, smiling and waving at the welcoming audience. In the middle of the stage, she slowly swirled, the lights catching like summer lightning on each gleaming spangle. A crystal appliqué flower clustered at her bosom, the shiny petals radiating out towards her tanned skin and smooth wide curls. The dress cascaded liquid glamour down her body. Vanna gazed into the spotlight as if it were just another sunrise. She was posture, grace, strong white teeth.

"Here's my favorite part," Jezebel said. "Every night, this moment is all about her. Can you imagine?"

Harlan tried. "No."

Vanna tilted her head as if to personally welcome Jezebel. A diamond cuff on her long toned arm glittered under the stage lights. She sparkled and glided into position, lighting up every corner, every edge, with her fingertips. She clapped softly, then folded her hands.

Jezebel clapped too, although her fingers seemed stiff. "You see that?" she murmured, pointing to the television. "That's beauty."

Jezebel's face absorbed the game show's glow. She seemed hungry and distant, which left a cold hole inside Harlan, a loss he imagined feeling if Jezebel left town, or got married, or died. Her brown eyes awaited like a drain, clogged by the flashing colors and wheel's turns. Harlan felt dizzy again. He rooted both his boots to the floor and promised himself he would not fall out of the chair in front of his baby sister.

"Buy a vowel! I! Get an I!" she screamed.

"She should get a U."

"She doesn't need the U when she has the I."

The phone rang. The contestant bought a U. The letter did not fit in the puzzle.

"I knew it!" Jezebel smirked at Harlan before she answered the phone. "Hey, Wade. Sure, come on by. Love ya." She turned back to the television.

"Wade coming over tonight?" asked Harlan.

"Yeah. Haven't seen much of him lately."

"Why?"

"He's pretty busy. Seems tired a lot."

Jezebel and Wade had been engaged for nine months, but they had yet to decide on flowers, get a dress, or even buy her a proper ring. The night Wade had proposed, Jezebel came home and waved her finger at Harlan. He'd been drinking during the day, but was sober enough to look for a sparkler on her finger. He saw nothing, except for what looked to be a piece of paper wrapped around her ring finger.

"Where's the ring?"

Jezebel had wiggled her fingers under his nose. "It's coming," she sang. "As soon as he sells three more cars, I get to pick out a ring!" She held her hand away from her, as if she were admiring two carats. "Till then, he gave me this."

Harlan grabbed her hand, studying her finger. It was a cigar band. His muscles flushed cold and his fingers clenched.

"Ain't nobody gives my little sister trash as a promise for forever," he said. "Where's he at?" He staggered towards the front door.

Jezebel shuffled between him and the door. "Get it together, Harlan!" She shoved him. The hounds sat up. "Why can't you just be happy for me, huh?"

"I am happy for you, Jezz." He focused with his good eye. "I'm just looking out for you."

"Yeah? You watching for me down the hollow of a bottle? And what do you see when you get to the bottom, Harlan?"

"If I'm lucky, nothin'."

"And that's exactly what you wanna see."

Harlan had been sucking from a handle of gin all day. The swirl of her words confused him, somehow stinging like a bee caught inside his collar.

Jezebel hoisted the gin bottle in the air. "I know why you drink so much, Harlan. 'Cuz you're afraid that when you get to the bottom, you'll be all alone."

Harlan was terrified she'd smash the bottle. It had cost him twenty-four dollars.

She peeled the label as if she were ripping out strands of hair. "You don't wanna be alone now that Mama's dead. Say it." Her face swelled red, her upper lip caught dry on her gums.

Harlan steadied himself with a dining room chair.

Jezebel tossed the shredded label around him like confetti at a surprise party. "Right, Harlan? You don't wanna drink your death like Mama, sneakin' it alone at night in the garage, do you?" The hounds barked when she raised her voice.

Where's my other bottle? He burned all over.

"Say it! Do you wanna be like Mama, Harlan? Cuz you're halfway there with that damn booze."

Harlan swiveled and punched through the wall. The hounds lunged, the bottle smashed. Jezebel grabbed their collars, dragging them away from Harlan. He seized the roll of paper towels to sop up the gin. He thought of twisting the wet paper towels over his mouth and letting the booze drip in, but was afraid Jezebel would forever see him in that moment, hating him with her hopeful blue eyes. Instead, he poured his garage stash over his bloodied knuckles and down his throat. The hounds whined. Harlan and Jezebel never spoke of it again, letting the incident dart away like a too-small fish not worth frying.

"What time is Wade coming?" asked Harlan.

"After this puzzle gets solved, I hope," said Jezebel. She tickled the hounds with ringless fingers.

"Well, it's time for me to work."

"See you in the morning. Got a big dive tomorrow. Gonna try for a minute forty-five under." She puffed out her cheeks. "Now if you'll 'scuse me, I gotta get back to the beautiful people, big brother." She bid him goodnight with a beauty pageant wave.

In the garage, Harlan reached behind his workbench and opened a beer. Cylinders and wires rested on the lids like dirty socks waiting to be folded. Harlan could refurbish any washing machine in the whole county, everyone knew that. So when a washer gave a last whir and its owner couldn't take one more short, the washer found itself dragged out to a curb with a sign that read "Take it, Harlan." He would troll the streets, loading these old washers into his pickup. Then he'd spend weeks breathing life into their frayed wires and clunking parts. Sometimes antiques dealers would buy the older washers. But he had to live, so Harlan also made house calls to fix newer washers.

Out front, a motorcycle pulled up to the house. Harlan didn't understand why Wade, a successful car salesman, wouldn't have a car. He didn't think it over too much, though, since it would make him burn with an angry thirst, and he never drank gin when finishing a job because he wanted to be sure about his work. Sometimes, though, a little beer lubricated the valves in his mind when he fiddled with inlet valves in a washer. He sipped the beer. He had to be accurate.

Mason's washing machine wasn't draining properly. Harlan had already checked the drain hose for kinks, already tested the lid timer. He tried another beer.

The water pump.

Harlan spent the next two hours labeling hoses, checking for blockages, and inspecting the impeller unit for damage. When he hooked it up to his tester hoses, water gushed into the tub, swirling in contained rapids. *My little river, my very own ocean. How beautiful.* It was beautiful enough to climb on in and take a dip.

Even in the garage, the hot night clutched like sweaty fingers around his neck. He stared into the metallic lake, regretting that he had never learned to swim. When the basket stopped spinning, he dipped his hand into the tub. The water was crisp and although it was clear, he envisioned it as the same scribbly blue of his old crayon drawings. Harlan kicked off his work boots. He climbed onto the lip of the machine, dangling his feet into the cool cartoon water. It lapped against his skin. Harlan celebrated his victories in home improvement with a gin chaser and a nap. He figured it wouldn't hurt anyone if he stayed in the water a while longer. He knew he wouldn't drown.

The morning pecked at Harlan's eyes.

"Harlan, you're gonna miss it," Jezebel hollered from the kitchen.

Harlan swung himself and his hangover out of bed. He didn't remember climbing out of his makeshift hot tub and under the covers. He stumbled into the kitchen. "Mornin'."

Wade stood shirtless at the stove, cooking eggs. "Hey, man."

Harlan felt a smile fall from his face like a loose hem. "Oh."

Jezebel bundled all her diving gear in a plastic grocery bag. "Big day today, I can feel it," she said. "Tide's 'bout to change." She sidled close to Wade and wrapped his arm around her shoulders. Her tan skin, her smile, her light eyes beamed. She looked like she was all lit up inside by some secret campfire.

"Speaking of," Wade said, "I'll get out at lunch today. How 'bout I stop by the shore?"

Jezebel tried to kiss him on the forehead but was too short, so she bounced up and got him on the eyelid instead. She seemed so happy.

The doorbell rang. Mason stood uneasy on the porch. "'Bout that time, Harlan. Show me what you got."

In the garage, Harlan was surprised to see he'd tidied up his tools and drained the washing machine. He stifled a relieved sigh as he demonstrated his repairs to Mason. The water shot from two separate hoses.

Mason grinned. "For all your hard work." He reached into his back pocket and handed Harlan an envelope of money. "Treat yourself something nice."

The two men loaded the washer onto Mason's flatbed. After he'd left, Harlan sat on his bed and counted the twenties. Two hundred dollars. He separated eighty into a manila envelope he kept hidden in his closet. That brought the total in the secret envelope to $891. His heart raced.

For the past year, Harlan had been stowing away money from his repairs to surprise Jezebel with a plane ticket all the way to Australia, where the last real pearl divers still practiced. Somewhere "off the northwestern coast of Broome." Jezebel had a map of it taped to her closet. If they were a religious bunch, the map would've been her priest, cross, and guardian angel all in one. She'd spend hours in her room, smiling at the map, tacking encyclopedia drawings of copper diving helmets and oyster beds over her chipped yellow walls. Harlan swore he even saw greasy lipstick marks on one of the pictures. Her boss, who owned the jewelry store, had visited Broome and photographed the divers from the shore. Jezebel told Harlan about it over pork chops one night.

"They go out in the dinghy at six in the morning and start diving around seven-thirty. Catch the low tide." She never seemed as happy as when she was either talking about diving or was in the water doing it, and in this moment, she couldn't even eat. "Then they're underwater in three hour shifts, scraping around down there for the most beautiful things in the world." She set her fork on her plate. "Harlan, I wanna be one of the people that gets to give something beautiful to everyone."

Harlan stopped chewing. "You already do, sis. Every day, here."

"Well, maybe I want something more. Don't you?"

Harlan had never thought about it. His whole life had presented itself to him draped in corduroy and flannel, and he accepted it without ever questioning why he still slept in his childhood bedroom or why his closest friends could be found behind the bar. He forgot a lot of other things too, like the name of the last girl he slept with, but he never forgot what Jezebel had said. That's when he started saving. I can do more than this, too, he announced to the gin bottles and washing machines. He couldn't pay much to bury his Mama, but he could try to help the one person who had ever helped him.

He shoved the wrinkled envelope behind the shoeboxes. The closet smelled like it always had, old and small.

The bell rang as Harlan entered the small humid store. All around him, bottles gleamed with mahogany rum or honeyed tequila. The vodkas looked more like water than eighty proof. Harlan ached.

"The usual, Harlan?"

"Yes, sir." Harlan handed over ten dollars for a fifth of their cheapest gin. "Thank you." His hands shook.

"Threw in some pretzels since you such a valued customer."

Harlan meandered back to the house along the riverbanks, stopping to drink and look at the azaleas. Then he spotted Jezebel, a bobbing dot on the river's liquid horizon. She gasped at the surface, dodging the floating branches and assorted trash.

A motorcycle roared to the shore, the dust dovetailing, dissipating. Harlan snuck closer so he could see with his good eye.

Jezebel trudged out of the water, pulling her feet through the mud. Beads of water sparkled on her body as if she was draped in strands of diamonds and pearls. Her bag sagged, empty.

Wade nodded at her from the bike and gripped the handlebars. "Girl, we gotta talk."

"You got a surprise for me?" She wiggled her ring finger.

Wade crossed his arms. "I'm strugglin'. Don't think I can do this anymore."

Jezebel gaped. The water streamed off her body like her skin was crying.

Harlan slapped at a mosquito he could hear but couldn't see.

"Sorry," Wade said. "But I been thinkin' 'bout it for the last seven months."

She covered her mouth. "Is there someone else?"

"Nah." Wade looked at the controls on his motorcycle. "You know me."

"Like hell."

He shrugged.

"So, this is how it ends," she said. "On a bike. On your lunch break."

"Don't matter when I did it. Just knew I had to."

"And you didn't even get off your bike, do it properly."

Harlan felt hot all over. He screwed the lid tight on his gin.

"I know, I'm a coward -"

She dropped her empty bag and backed away from him. Her face cracked. She tore from Wade and ran toward the house. The hounds sprinted with her. Wade shook his head and started his engine.

Harlan tucked his gin inside the paper bag and strode out from the bushes. The rock he threw at Wade's disappearing image landed in the dead dry leaves.

When Harlan staggered into the house, Jezebel was doubled over in the kitchen, clutching her stomach, sobbing the way she did at Mama's funeral. Harlan's guts dropped.

"You're soaked."

"How did that happen?" she wheezed.

Don't cry like that. I want to get loaded when you do that. He tried to focus.

"Where does it all go?" Her mouth looked like a slash across her face.

Harlan rubbed her back, squeezing away the tears in his own eyes. *Please stop.* "I'll kill him, Jezebel, I swear to God I'll kill him."

"No," she screamed. "Don't be stupid." She clutched at his sleeve.

"I ain't stupid, Jezebel." *I ain't.*

In the garage, Harlan shoved his workbench across the floor and gathered all the beers he had hidden. He shotgunned five of them. The beer hotfooted its way into his head, his fingers, his rage. Then he pocketed a flask of gin and walked the half-mile to the local saloon. *Nobody hurts my sister.* Harlan and his gin stormed into town.

He knew both the bartenders at the Bucking Bronco, and even stuffed himself silly at their Thanksgiving buffet one year. Inside the bar, it smelled of bleach and half-licked peanut shells. Harlan took a stool on the end. The bartender nodded and poured him the usual, three shots of their cheapest gin. Harlan settled into his shots.

He had a ritual of lining them up, from fullest to smallest. That way, by the time he got to the last one, he was already drinking less. He used to do it by color, darkest to lightest, back when he would mix tequila, rum and vodka. He called them his grab bag shots. But now he stuck to gin, which got the job done quick. Harlan had already taken the first two shots when his ear snagged a conversation behind him.

"That's right baby, grab my stick!"

Harlan froze.

"Watch the blue balls!"

Harlan turned. At the pool table in the corner, Wade leaned into a laughing blonde. She was a column of tossed hair, brazen giggles, arched back. Wade kissed her neck.

Harlan took his last shot and then bore towards the pool table. He squinted with his good eye and shoved Wade from behind. Before Wade could respond, Harlan socked him in the back of his head. The blonde screamed. Harlan punched again, missed, squinted, and hooked Wade's chin on the backspin. *Ain't nobody hurts Jezebel.*

"Ain't nobody, ain't nobody," Harlan wailed. He punched his knuckles slick, splitting. He was carbon. Feral.

A black boot nailed Harlan in the stomach. He gasped, lurching off Wade. Every nerve in his back exploded. Then a fist barreled into his good eye and he felt dragged by his hair through some kind of internal tunnel where he couldn't see, couldn't breathe, couldn't stop. The room spun and something wet hit Harlan's cheek.

"You bastard," a woman shrieked. Spit landed on him again. "I pity your mama for makin' trash like you."

Wade groaned nearby.

"Don't be stupid now," someone with a stern voice said into Harlan's ear. He couldn't see who it was, but he felt his arms being pinned behind him. "You have the right to remain silent." Two plastic zip ties rigged his wrists together. Someone stood him upright. Harlan's good eye tried to focus as he moved forward into the dusk. Outside, the headlights shone like pearls poised to roll out of their shells.

Harlan was a tadpole swimming at the surface of a dream. Jezebel, large, white, kind, swam through the river next to him. Harlan shot ahead. Then he was scooped into a bag filled with water. He could see the hard dry world beyond the skin of the bag, bright and blue and green. He darted in nervous circles.

Soon it was dark, cool. His world poured down in a smooth cascade of water. He gasped.

"Don't worry, little tadpole," Jezebel called. "I'll save you." She pushed a button.

A waterfall rumbled. Cold water filled the darkness. Harlan relaxed and swam. Around and around.

Then everything began to shake. Harlan couldn't see it, couldn't stop it. But just by the feel of it, he knew.

He awoke with a full bladder and what felt like at least one broken rib. He swallowed, his tongue coated with the residue of bad memories that had yet to return in full force. Through the bars, he saw a clock. It was eleven minutes after seven in the evening. A vein throbbed somewhere behind his good eye, so he pressed his fingers against it to make it stop.

"Warden," Harlan yelled. His stomach churned with the effort.

A man in an office leaned his head out. "Whatcha want?"

"I hafta take a leak."

"Turn around and do it then. Ain't nothin' I wanna see."

Harlan hadn't even thought to turn around. Every muscle in his neck felt too tight, like rubber bands poised to snap against skin. He closed his eyes and inhaled, twisting slowly on the exhale until a dull silver toilet, a rim really, came into view. He pushed himself upright, swallowing the burning spit-bile that comes before getting sick. The cell, the bars, the slick floor all bent and expanded with each step. He collapsed on the toilet, his head spinning in his hands. He held on tight so it wouldn't whirl away.

"You done?" asked the warden.

Harlan wanted to sleep right there, curled up like a deflated punchball. The rim felt good against his thighs, and he thought about what he wouldn't give to let his body slide down to the floor so he could rest his pounding forehead against the cool metal. But instead, he pulled up his pants and stumbled towards the voice. "Yes, sir."

"Good. Either you post bail or you make yourself comfy. You choose. You can make your phone call right now."

Harlan was afraid that more than words would come out if he spoke. "How much is bail?"

"Nine hundred bucks."

Harlan winced. Everything spun. He gripped the bars.

The warden unlocked the holding cell and walked Harlan to a phone. "You get one."

Harlan stared at the shiny metal phone, thinking about what to say. The room was hot, save for a tiny desk fan that blew about as hard as a cat's exhale. Sweat dribbled down the small of his back. He didn't want to talk, didn't want the heat from his stale breath to add to the warmth in the room. His fingers cramped as he dialed.

"Can you hear me, Jezebel?" *Wheel of Fortune* echoed in the background.

"You okay?" She sounded breathy.

"I'm still standing." Harlan closed his eyes to stop the spinning. "But I'm in jail."

Jezebel gasped.

His mouth was an overstuffed pillow. "I need you. In the back of my closet, behind them shoeboxes is a envelope of money. Now, I might need to borrow ten from you. But there got to be enough money in that envelope to post bail." The world spun away from him like a kite in a tornado. "Please bring it here, Jezz." His good eye swelled shut.

She set the phone down to find the envelope. Harlan could hear the chimes from the game show, light and hopeful. He wondered what Vanna was wearing but flinched at the idea of all her shining sequins.

"It's in my hands," Jezebel said and hung up.

I'm not stupid. I'm not.

"All done?" The warden escorted Harlan past the mirrored office, back to the holding cell.

Harlan caught a glimpse of his face, scabbed and swollen. "Looks like."

Jezebel picked him up in the old silver Sebring, her eyes focused on anything other than his. "I dunno know how you done got all that money. Don't wanna know. But I'm proud you didn't drink it."

Harlan gagged whenever he opened his mouth or his eyes, so he concentrated on not getting sick out the window. Remnants from the hot afternoon still nagged at the air, even this late in the evening.

"I'm sorry I pulled you outta your show tonight," he said.

"Always gonna be another."

The car air was stagnate with heat and silence, creeping in at all angles and refusing to move. After she'd passed their street, Harlan gripped his kneecaps and forced his mouth to speak.

"Where you goin' Jezz?"

"To the edge."

She pulled the car, a little too fast, through the dogwoods to an old childhood swimming hole. The sunset oozed on the horizon like a cracked quail egg. Jezebel reached down at his feet, yanking her plastic bag from under his boot.

Harlan groaned. His guts felt snagged behind him the way a t-shirt catches on a tree branch. "I can't get up."

"Then you get to sit there and watch."

The night exhaled resignation into the already warm car. Harlan watched his sister maneuver through the flickering waves of heat towards the river's edge, the empty bag trailing behind her like the train on a gown. He watched and watched, until she was just a muted sparkle against the curve of the searing sun, a little flare streaming out of the horizon, a bag billowing, a woman diving.

KERRY DONOGHUE RECEIVED HER MFA FROM THE UNIVERSITY OF SAN FRANCISCO IN 2008.

EMAIL: KDONOGHUE9@HOTMAIL.COM.

THE LONG WAY HOME
BY DREW McCOY

I

The two men sat on the front porch in cane back chairs in the twilight hour of early morning. The sky grey with the hint of rain, the temperature steadily rising before them as they sat, the waves of heat though unseen were beginning to ripple out there along the horizon. The trees in front of the house were shrouded in darkness and the men could not make out their shape nor their leaf filled limbs rattling in the stiff wind, the smell of rain trailing on the tail end of the breeze. Their coffee sat steaming atop a small pinewood table and neither man spoke for a long moment.

Your daddy gets out today, the old man said, rocking in the chair.

Boyd nodded and turned to his granddaddy. It's been a long eight years, he said.

The old man said nothing. He took up the nearest mug and sipped the coffee.   Boyd picked up the other mug and stared into its contents, the black liquid swirling with the slightest movement. You want to ride out there with me, Boyd said.

To pick up your daddy?

Yeah.

The old man made a noise like a laugh and shook his head no. I'll see him when he gets into town.

You think he'll come by and visit?

Hard to say.

Yeah, it's all too hard to say.

Evelyn going with you, the old man said.

No. She says she ain't ready to see him just yet.

Not sure anybody is.

Guess it don't matter much either way because in a few hours he's back in all of our lives.

The old man nodded and drank from the chipped, stained mug of coffee. Boyd watched the old man, studied his actions and manners and stared at his wrinkled skin which resembled sun aged corn husks. His hair remained black as raven feathers and wiry. The old man was getting older. He did not move like he used to and when he did he shuffled and limped as if his bones would not bend properly. Boyd stood from the chair and crossed the porch. The floorboards creaked under his boots. He withdrew a battered pack of cigarettes from his breastpocket and shook one loose and lit it and blew the match out. He leaned against the porch railing and looked out at the darkness and smoked. He had not seen nor spoken to his father in eight years and in just a few moments he'd be driving out to the prison to reclaim his father and bring him home or what was left of it. He stubbed out the cigarette on the porch railing and turned back to the old man.

You think he's changed any?

In looks or attitude?

Both, Boyd said and shrugged.

Knowing your daddy I'd say neither.

Me too. Boyd crossed the porch again and eased himself in the cane back chair, leaned back, crossed his legs.

The two men sat in silence, the world lighting up all around them with the ascent of the sun, the grey clouds backlit a pale yellow. They drank their coffee and sat, both men staring out off the porch across the dew laden yard to the woodlot near the driveway entrance. Nothing there to be seen save trees of live oaks, poplars and maples, their limbs full of green leaves, squirrels racing across the branches, jumping from tree to tree, barking noisily at one another.

You think your mama knows what today is? The old man was not looking at Boyd; instead he was looking down at the antique bone handled one blade pen knife he was fiddling with, using the pen blade to dig underneath his fingernails.

Boyd shrugged. Said, I don't know. I'd say though that wherever she is she's looking over her shoulder, wondering if he'll come looking for her.

The old man nodded. You think he will?

Go looking for her?

Yeah.

No. Not if he knows what's best for him he won't.

You going to tell him about Jimmy?

Boyd shrugged and drank from the mug of coffee.

You need to, the old man said then. He clasped the pen knife shut and looked up at Boyd. You know that right?

I know it.

When you leaving? The old man's voice a mixture of cigarettes and whiskey, it reminded Boyd of gravel and the deep hills of Kentucky the man was born of, the deep piney woods that were instilled in the old man, running thick in him like blood.

Here in a bit, Boyd said. It's a good ways out there.

Be sure to call me before he comes up here.

I will.

The old man stood and half walked half shuffled to the steps. I just don't want him coming over here when I ain't ready for him.

I understand, Boyd said and stood. He twirled the keys to his pickup on his finger and walked down the rickety porch steps for the truck.

Drive safe, the old man said, tipping his mug at Boyd's departure. Boyd nodded and walked down the steps two at a time into the grey light of morning as the moon dropped below the horizon and the sun began to rise and crest the eastern tree lined horizon.

He turned in the old man's gravel driveway and pulled out onto the main road, not once looking back at the small house nor the old man, who remained standing there like a statue, watching Boyd drive off, watching the dust of the dirt road rise and then fade. The truck Boyd drove had at one time been the old man's and it was battered and rusted along the wheel wells and running boards and there was no power steering, no cruise control and the radio was busted, wires hanging from the dashboard like tentacles. It was going to be a long drive. He drove the truck in fifth gear, speeding down the empty two lane road. He passed the town still shrouded in darkness, then further away from town, nestled against woodlots and stands of pine trees farmhouse windows unlit and cloaked in the purple darkness of dawn.

He drove further down the highway with the rising sun at his back and the waning light from the previous evening quickly fading into the redness of the new day. The rising sun and the clouds fanning across the morning sky were striated yellow and orange. He studied the sky for a long moment, allowing his mind to briefly stray from the day's plan and become lost in the beauty of this new day, lost on the tails of clouds as they sifted and glided across the sky.

He rode in silence with the air conditioner thumbed all the way and still the interior of the truck remained hot. He cranked the windows down. He gripped the wheel with both hands as the wind blew stiff from left to right jolting the truck on its aging shocks. He wanted this day over with before it had even started. Far against the horizon a tractor trolled soundlessly, brown puffs of dirt rising in its wake, marking it for Boyd to track as it followed the straightness of the flat horizon. He had dreamed of his father the previous night and in this dream his father walked among Boyd and his mother in a field of golden wheat. In the dream it was summer and the sun shone bright and orange upon their pale winter faces. He did not know the meaning of the dream and the dream therefore was foreign and so were the people and the expressions on the peoples faces were foreign too. The land in the dream was not a land Boyd had ever stepped foot. The horizon of the land in the dream was cropped and jagged with snowcapped peaks of tall mountains. It was not home nor would it ever be.

He blinked the images of the dream away and concentrated on the stretch of road that lay ahead. In the distance he saw a man standing on the edge of the road, his thumb stuck in the air. This man appeared out of the mist and fog of the morning like an apparition and as Boyd neared he waited for the man's existence to dissolve back into the summer morning and for the road to be clear, just him and it. But the man went no where. He stood on the gravel apron of the road with the wind whipping at his pants legs, blowing up loose pieces of trash and roadside debris. He wore a brown hat and jacket and slung over his shoulder was a green surplus bag. Boyd slowed the truck and leaned and rolled down the window.

Where you headed?

The man was not a man so much as he was a boy. Boyd figured his age to fall in or near early twenties. The boy looked up. His face was red and chaffed from the summer heat.

Not too far, the boy said. Just an hour up the road.

Boyd nodded. Hop in.

The boy's green surplus bag sat between Boyd and the boy on the bench seat. It smelled of sweat and soiled clothes and stale cigarette smoke. Boyd studied the boy out of the corner of his eye. They boy looked tired and beat down as if the road had laid itself upon him.

What's your name? Boyd asked.

Josh, the boy said.

I'm Boyd. He extended a hand and they shook and the boy's hand was calloused and streaked with dirt and sweat.

Boyd slid the air conditioner dial back and forth a few times. Doesn't work like it used too.

Seems to work just fine, the boy said. Anything's better than standing out there in that dang heat.

I bet, Boyd said.

Where you headed to, the boy Josh said to Boyd.

Boyd hissed air through his pursed lips. He took a deep breath, thinking of the right way to tell it, if he were to tell it at all.

To pick up my daddy, he said.

The boy nodded like he knew there was more. Where's he at?

He's down in Manchester. Today's his release date.

The boy shook his head slowly then turned and stared out the window at the passing land.

They rode for miles in silence past long forgotten farms whose barns lay crumpled and misshapen under tarnished tin roofs shrouded in kudzu and wild weeds. They drove past summer fed fields, past fields of lush corn where the golden husks shone brightly in the morning sun.

What'd he do? the boy asked a moment later.

My daddy?

Yeah.

What didn't he do, Boyd said, then, he shot somebody.

He kill em?

Yeah, he killed them.

The boy Josh nodded slightly then he raised his hands in front of the vents then he dangled his right hand loosely out the open window.

What about you? Boyd asked.

The boy shrugged.

You off to meet somebody?

Not sure, really. Just needed to get away from my last place is all.

I understand.

Boyd took the next exit and drove until he found a gas station. He pulled the truck up to the first pump and cut the engine and opened the door. The boy sat up in the seat, smoothed down his disshelved hair.

Let me pay for the gas, the boy said.

Boyd shook his head no. I was driving this way with or without you.

For your daddy, the boy said to himself more than to Boyd.

For my daddy, Boyd said. He stepped out of the truck, his boots crunching on the loose bits of dirt and gravel. It was hot and the air was laden with moisture that stuck to Boyd's skin like another layer all together draped atop his clothes.

The boy Josh climbed out of the truck then slid his bag across the seat and shrugged it on his shoulder and straightened his pants. He walked around the back of the truck and leaned against the tailgate and fender.

Thank you for the ride, he said.

Boyd looked up from the gas nozzle. This is it?

Yep, this is it. I can walk it from here.

Boyd looked around. There was nothing to see save the gas station and the few trucks and their drivers still sleeping from the previous night. The sun was above the horizon now, spreading widely about the afternoon sky. To the west the sky was filled with blueblack clouds that rolled and tumbled across the grey sky.

Boyd shrugged then nodded. He reached out and shook the boy's hand. Be careful, okay? It looks like it might rain.

Okay. I will. The boy turned and walked towards the two lane road in front of the gas station. He looked back once and told Boyd thanks again and Boyd nodded and waved. He stood there awhile even after the tank was filled watching the boy walk away, he missed the boy's company already.

Boyd paid the man behind the counter with cash. He went to the restroom in the back of the building and pissed and washed his hands. When he came out of the bathroom he smelt bacon and sausage and fresh coffee. Further down the narrow hall past the ladies restroom tucked into the back of the gas station was a room with a long counter with stools and behind the counter was an open kitchen with a grill where a black man in a grease stained apron flipped thick sausage patties and cracked eggs onto the grills. The diner was small and aligned against the walls were booths with laminate tops. The black man turned and nodded at Boyd and said nothing. Boyd nodded back and raised his hand weakly, waved. The diner was empty save for a pair of grizzly looking truck drivers, each sitting at the counter eating eggs and grits. Boyd turned and left and walked back outside to the truck. He cranked the engine and headed down the road towards the boy.

The boy had not made it far up the road. Boyd slowed the truck and eased it onto the apron of the road. He rolled up next to him.

Get in, Boyd said, leaning across the bench seat.

The boy Josh looked up at Boyd puzzled then he smiled faintly.

Get in, Boyd said again. There's a diner back up the road.

Boyd stepped on the brake and the truck lurched forward to a halt. Still leaning across the bench seat with his left hand he opened the passenger side door. The boy Josh shook his head and laughed. He tossed his bag into the back of the truck and climbed in.

You hungry?

Yes, sir, the boy said.

Good, because this place has some mean looking sausage.

They sat in a far corner booth away from the grill and entrance. Just the two of them now, the truck drivers gone, their plates already cleared, the smoke from their cigarettes long faded into the smoke from the grill. The black man did not acknowledge them when they entered so they seated themselves wherever they liked. They sat in silence as they waited on the waitress. Boyd smoked and sat staring at the boy, trying to place him, trying without asking or prying to decipher the boy's past. Make some sense of why he was where he was at this point of his life. Looking straight ahead at the boy Boyd saw that his eyes were green and clear and this small fact in itself put Boyd at ease because he believed clear eyes, eyes void of distraction, meant a clear head.

A middle aged woman wearing a blue denim shirt with brown curly hair streaked with grey stood over the table. She pulled a pencil from behind her ear and flipped the order pad in her other hand.

What can I get you gentleman, she said, her voice thick with years of smoke.

I'll have sausage and eggs with a biscuit, Boyd said. A cup of coffee.

And you, she said, turning towards the boy.

Uh, just give me the same.

She did not bother to write down their order. She walked away and leaned on the counter and told their order to the black man working the grill.

She looks like my mom, the boy said.

The waitress?

Yeah.

She's attractive then, your mom is.

She was.

Where is she now?

Don't know, the boy said. She ran off with her boyfriend when I was twelve. Haven't seen her since.

That's too bad, Boyd said. She's missing out on a good young man.

She wouldn't have cared. Her boyfriend, Lenny, he was a meth dealer. Always cooking the stuff in our trailer, not caring about me or brother. Anyways I was glad to see her go.

I'm sorry.

Don't be. It was for the better.

They sat in silence. Boyd smoked and drank his coffee. The diner was empty still, as if it was only open for Boyd and the boy Josh.

You ever try it?

Meth? Boyd said.

Yeah.

No, no. Never have. You?

No, the boy said. Not after I watched it tear apart my family.

The waitress returned with their food and coffee. The food was served on heavy plates of white china aged with years of food stains. The mugs of coffee were solid, thick and hot to the touch. The eggs were smothered in butter and salt and pepper and the biscuits glistened with butter and grease. The two of them ate and drank wordless and without expression and someone just walking into the diner would be safe to assume that they were father and son and not two lost, wandering strangers. When the boy was finished he wiped his mouth with the cloth napkin and pushed his plate aside and rested his hands atop the laminate tabletop.

What's with the stuff in the back of the truck?

Boyd looked up from the steaming food then he rested the forkful of eggs on the edge of the plate and sat up.

It's nothing really, he said. Just some stuff for my brother.

You have a brother?

Boyd nodded. Haven't seen him a while, but, to answer your question, yeah I have a brother. In fact you kind of remind me of him.

How come you haven't seen him?

Boyd rolled around the possible answers in his head and when he could not settle upon just one he simply looked at the boy sitting across from him and said, He just moved on from here. Two people going two different directions.

Like me and my mom, the boy Josh said. And Boyd knew it was not a question but merely the boy stating some realization aloud for the first time.

Back in the truck driving west, the sky dark before them with storms and lightning flashing near the edge of the distant horizon, the clouds glowing yellowwhite then back to purple, the world around them slowly slipping away to a darkness that appeared malevolent. The boy Josh reminded Boyd of his brother, Jimmy. Not in appearance or movement but in the way the boy viewed the world, with a sense of naivety mingled with a notion of realism that life is hard, but somehow walking through it all with a smile on his face. They hadn't spoken since leaving the diner and the boy Josh sat slouched in the bench seat with this head turned towards the window, his forehead resting against the threshold, the warm wind a rush of sanity upon his face.

They drove past signs for small towns Boyd hadn't a name for, some he'd never heard of before. They drove on past vast amounts of empty land where cattle grazed in the open pastures on dry grass and beyond the pastures the glint of a distant river winding and cutting its way across the land. There were no homes this far west just woodlots and stands of cedars and woods of pine trees. The land flattened and the road widened and on either side of the road were fields of corn and tobacco and soy stretching far as the eye could see, to the horizon it seemed, where their shape dropped over the lip of it.

Do you have money? Boyd asked then, breaking the silence.

The boy nodded.

You have enough?

Yes, sir. I'm pretty sure I do.

What will you do?

I don't rightly know just yet. Figure I'll keep going west though, there's bound to be something out there waiting for me.

Boyd was still hours from Manchester and the prison and although the boy's company had been a welcomed distraction from what still lied ahead it still remained that Boyd had to deal with his father the morning following, a man he had not seen in eight years, a man he had spoken to on the phone a handful of times in the past eight years, a man he had quit calling his father eight years ago.

How far you want to go? Boyd turned and looked at Josh. He was sitting upright, his arm rested on the open window.

However far you're willing to go, he said back.

I think I'll stop soon, Boyd said. I still got some hours till Manchester and that weather isn't looking promising. Boyd raised his finger from atop the steering wheel, pointed at the darkening sky that awaited them, the blooming lightning above the cloud laden horizon.

Wherever you stop is fine by me, the boy said.

The motel parking lot was vacant save a few cars and a tractor trailer rig. It was set just off the main road. The motel's office was a building made of wood and years before it had been poorly painted red and yellow, the red now faded to a soft pink, the yellow nearly white. He parked the truck in front of the office and cut the engine and cranked the windows up then opened the door and stepped down. His back was stiff and his legs ached from the long ride. He was hot and sweaty, his shirt soaked and sticking to his back and shoulders. Beads of sweat formed and rolled down his brow past his eyes and into his mouth, the salty flavor sour and distasteful.

The boy Josh was seated on the lowered tailgate, his green bag in his hands. He stood when Boyd came around the back of the truck.

I can get you a room, Boyd said. You can shower; take a nap if you want.

That's okay, the boy said. I appreciate the offer though. I really do.

Boyd did not argue with the boy because he could hear it in the boy's words, the readiness he spoke of to step into the real world, an excitement Boyd had not seen in a person in a long time, if ever. Standing behind the truck in front of the motel office they shook hands one final time then the boy Josh turned for the road. Boyd stood there a long time watching the boy walk away, his arms down by his sides. He watched until the figure of the boy was silhouetted against the dark clouds then as the boy was a mere dark spot on the horizon then gone. As if he were never there, like Jimmy, Boyd thought to himself.

He had not planned on stopping but the events of the day led him to the cheap motel. And the room was hot and fetid and smelt of smoke. There was a pair of ragged pale curtains stretched across the lone square window, the last light of day faintly seeped through them spreading across the room's carpeted floor in weak bands. Dust motes floating in and out of the light. He called Evelyn to tell her that he had stopped for the night. He did not tell her about the boy Josh. Then he called the prison, told the woman working the phones that he'd be there tomorrow, early in the morning to claim his father.   Done talking to people he returned the phone back in the cradle and undressed and folded his clothes and set them atop the bed. Naked, he crossed the room to the bathroom where he pulled back the molded plastic shower curtain and turned on the water. He showered under cold water, letting the steel cold feeling of it swath his body frigid until goose bumps rose on his bare, naked skin.

He toweled himself dry, running the towel through his black hair then he wrapped the towel around his waist and went back to the room. And sat on the bed, the damp towel cool and wet against his skin, and stared blankly at the TV and walls, the wallpaper peeling and unrolling in the corners of the room. He stood and crossed the room and fingered back one of the curtains. The dropping sun was shrouded behind greyblack clouds, slipping behind the rim of the earth, a burnt fiery trail in its wake backlighting the clouds purpleblue. Darkness would soon come and overtake the day and Boyd would try to sleep. Pale white lightning bloomed and dispersed soundlessly across the night sky then it was dark again with no moon, just the light from the streetlamp offering only a pitiful rounded shaft of light. There was no rain yet but Boyd could smell it in the air and the wind was coming, running through the tops of the live oak trees bordering the side of the motel. He could hear it rustling through the drooping leaves, the leaves weighed down with brown dust and dirt from the parking lot and nearby drouted fields.

He lay atop the bed bare chested, clothed only in his underwear. A feeling of dread weighed in his stomach. He was hot and the room was hot. He thought of his father, of the last time they saw each other a day before he shot and killed that man. Boyd had not attended the trial, if one could even call it that. His father pleaded guilty, acted as if he were proud of what he had done, and welcomed the prison sentence. He closed his eyes but sleep eluded him and could do nothing but allow his mind to turn up lost images of his youth, when Jimmy and he were just boys, playing shirtless in the backyard of their house, their mother on the porch drinking iced tea watching her two sons play in the day's of summer. Such a long time ago the memories seemed foreign, as if they were altogether someone else's. After a while he slept.

I I

They drove away from the prison in Boyd's weathered black pick up in the early morning with the windows down. The warm outside air rushed in and blew about on their faces and necks. The barbed-wire fences and guard towers loomed ominously in the rearview mirror and not once did either man look back at them as they drove on towards home.

Boyd watched the blackened woods pass as he drove the truck along the grey stretch of road, the day's heat shimmering above it in layered waves. On the bench seat sat a tattered cardboard box. Contained in it were his father's belongings: a gold watch that no longer kept the time, a battered pack of cigarettes and a tarnished silver Zippo.

His father had been waiting on him just inside the prison gate that morning, the prison issued box tucked under his arm, a cigarette dangling from his crooked mouth. He looked older, feebler; the eight years away had not been kind and Boyd tried to find some empathy for the man he called his father but he could find none.

Didn't think you'd be the one picking me up, his father said.

Me neither.

Figured I'd see your mama waiting on me.

She couldn't make it.

Couldn't or wouldn't?

Both, Boyd said. Wouldn't.

His father smiled at this. How's she doing?

She's remarried.

His father laughed out of the corner of his mouth. We were never divorced.

He's good to her, Boyd said.

Well, she always deserved better.

We all did, Boyd said back.

His father removed a cigarette from the pack and lit it with a match; he shook the match out and leaned his head back and smoked.

Her new man keeping up with the farm?

Boyd shook his head no. She moved away with him.

His father rubbed his hand through his thinning black hair and shook his head slowly. Where?

Up north. And don't go looking for her.

Your mama?

Boyd nodded.

Why not?

She's scared.

Of what?

Of what you might do to her new man.

He took a long pull from the cigarette and exhaled and the smoke hung like a cloud in front of his face. Now what would I do to him?

Boyd turned his eyes away from the road and looked at his father. Kill him.

I ain't going to kill nobody, his father said. Your mama knows that and hell it didn't work out too good the last time I did it either.

How's pop doing?

Boyd looked over at his father, studied him a long moment before speaking. How the two men looked so similar, their hawk billed noses, their black hair and eyebrows and broad shoulders. But their eyes, the old man's were tender and warm and his father's eyes were cold and grey the color of gunmetal.

He's getting by, Boyd said then.

Still collecting his pension?

Boyd nodded and rested his left elbow on the lip of the open window, steered the truck with his right hand.

We going up to see him?

He wants us to call first.

His father shook his head and cursed. He drew hard on the cigarette then exhaled, releasing the smoke out effortlessly then he flicked it out the open window and onto the road.

The sun was beginning to rise above the dark rim of the horizon as they pushed on towards home and the eastern sky burned with an orange tint. They drove on for miles in a dead silence.

His father eyed the plastic thermos that was rolling back and forth on the floorboard between his son's feet. Coffee?

Yeah.

Mind if I have some?

Don't see no reason why not.

Boyd reached for the thermos and passed it to his father and his father unscrewed the lid and poured its contents into the cup. He drank it in gulps. Best damn thing I've tasted in eight years.

I bet, Boyd said, more to himself than to his father.

Where we going?

Boyd shrugged. Wherever you want.

Any bars open this early?

You're serious?

Yeah.

What do you want?

Alcohol, son. Beer, whiskey, hell a glass of fucking wine would do about now.

Not sure that's a good idea.

Well when have I ever had any good ideas?

Boyd said nothing in response and they drove on without talking and the western sky through the rearview mirror darkened finally with the threat of rain. They drove past fields of corn and tobacco and empty pastures save the grain silos and barns with tin roofs and the land in this part of the state was barren and dry from the months without rain.

Boyd steered the truck into the parking lot, the gravel crunched loudly under the tires. The parking lot was empty save two other automobiles, a car and truck, and if he had to guess he would have said the red beat up Chevy Capri belonged to the waitress and he guessed the white Ford with the fancy mud flaps belonged to the owner.

You sure this is what you want? Boyd asked his father, killing the ignition.

I'm sure, his father said then he opened the door and stepped down from the truck. He stretched and popped his neck and back several times before closing the door.

Hand me those smokes, his father said through the open window.

Boyd grabbed the cigarettes and climbed out of the truck himself. His father was leaning against the side of the truck with his foot propped on the tire just under the wheel well and he was staring with great intent at the wreath of flowers lying in the bed of the truck and the two shovels that were stacked on top of a large folded tarpaulin. His father looked up and Boyd held his father's gaze for a long moment, daring him to ask and when he did not Boyd walked past him into the bar.

They had their pick of where to sit and his father idled up at the first bar stool he came upon. The bar was empty and dark save the early morning sun slanting through the pane window.

You want anything when she comes over? his father asked.

Boyd shook his head no.

You sure? Because I'm buying. His father removed a crumpled twenty dollar bill from his pants pocket and laid it on the table and smoothed it out the best he could.

You men are early this morning, a woman said. She was standing behind them and both men turned around on their bar stools to see her. We just unlocked the door a minute or two ago.

His father smiled at the woman and his eyes looked her up from her boots to her brown hair. Well ain't you a pretty little thing.

The woman did not smile nor did she say anything back in response, she just walked around them and lifted a section of the bar and stepped through. Reflected in the bar mirror Boyd could see his father's cold, steel eyes and his crooked hellish grin then Boyd looked at himself and shook his head slowly.

What do you want? the woman said.

A cold beer and a glass of whiskey, his father said.

What kind of whiskey?

Jim Beam, Jack. Hell whatever you got open will do, his father said.

You, she said, nodding to Boyd.

Nothing.

The woman turned her back to father and son and poured the two drinks.

When she returned his father tossed back the shot of whiskey and smoked. He slid the crumpled twenty across the counter, expecting change. He kept the same grin as before on his face the entire time and it was a grin Boyd had seen on his father's face from years past. No good had ever come from it.

How come you never came and visited me up there?

Guess I was trying to move on.

You can't move on from blood son. I'm your daddy and I'll be your daddy till the day you die. You can't escape that.

It was worth a try.

His father lit another cigarette with the lit end of the one he was just smoking then he dropped that one in the empty whiskey glass and it hissed when it reached the bottom.

They sat in silence. The woman behind the bar moved about as if Boyd and his father were not there. She wiped down glasses with a white dish towel all the while whistling a tune Boyd could not decipher.

How's the little one doing? his father said a while later.

Good, Boyd said. She's getting tall, taking after her mom.

When can I see her?

She doesn't want you around her.

Your wife?

Yeah.

I'm the little girl's grandfather.

I know.

Then tell her that.

I tried.

That goddamn wife of yours.

Don't bring her into this.

It's because of what they said I did, isn't it?

Boyd nodded.

Don't believe those judges and lawyers, his father said. It was self-defense.

Not how the jury saw it.

Fuck the jury. It should've been a mistrial. Damn prosecutor's fourth cousin sat on that jury.

Don't start that again, Boyd said in disgust. A man was found dead and you had the gun. Not hard to put the pieces together.

It was a long time ago.

Yeah it was, Boyd said. Eight years.

What do you want from me? You want me to say I'm sorry for all the shit I've done? Is that it?

Boyd said nothing back, he just stared at the far wall lined with bottles of bourbon and whiskey and vodka and all he could think of was how all those bottles contributed to the reason he was were he was: sitting in a bar with his ex convict of a father.

His father took a long drink from his beer then he set the glass down and looked at his son. I can't change the past, he said. What's done is done.

Boyd stood from the booth and walked wordlessly to the bathroom in the back of the bar. The bathroom was small and dingy and smelt of urine and stale beer. The floor was sticky and wet. There was a single window above the paper towel dispenser that offered only a pitiful wedge of light to spread across the tiled floor. He stepped over the puddles and into the single stall that bore no door. He sat on the toilet and clasped his hands in his lap and read the inscriptions on the walls of the stall as if they might hold some great meaning and when no meaning revealed itself he stood to face his father, again.

His father grinned and threw back the last of the beer.

I thought a lot about you while I was away, his father said.

Yeah, Boyd said. Did you think about that other family you ruined?

More about my own and how much I've wronged you and your brother.

Don't say his name.

Who? Jimmy?

I told you not to speak his name.

Where's he lay his head these days?

He's around, Boyd said without expression.

You take me to see him?

I don't know.

Shit, Boyd he's my son. I have a right to see my son.

I know it.

Then you'll take me over?

Boyd nodded yes and stood. He waved to the barkeep and nodded thanks and turned for the door, not waiting on his father.

Boyd stood outside the bar in the faint morning light and the sky was now a crowded mess of towering greyblack clouds and soundless lightning franticly streaked across the sky. The wind was picking up, turning the backs of the leaves pale and running through them like quicksilver. His father exited the bar a moment later, a cigarette between his two fingers, the smoke trailing in his wake like exhaust.

Jimmy still living off Cypress Trail?

No, Boyd said, patting his pants pockets for the keys. He's at the old hunting cabin. Been back there a few months now.

What the hell is he doing living out there?

Boyd shrugged and opened the door to the truck and climbed in and cranked the engine, never looking away from the sky. You coming or not?

The cabin was dark and musty and cobwebs dangled loosely from the ceiling like ribbons from some long ago party.

Jimmy's living in this shit hole?

More or less.

What does that mean?

Here, Boyd said. Give me a hand opening this.

It was an old ice chest that his father recognized immediately, his eyes wide with it. Where did you get that?

Just help me get it open.

It took both of them to lift open the large heavy door and when they did a burst of cold air rushed over their faces and both men took a step back not only from the cold air but from what awaited them.

Inside the ice chest was Jimmy, his body frozen in the fetal position. His brown hair was stiff and cold and small clear slivers of ice hung like daggers from the strands of it and from his mustache and goatee. His face and lips were pale blue and his eyes were open and void of expression and when Boyd rolled his brother over his father stared directly into those lifeless eyes and he could muster no words to speak to his dead son. His father shuddered.

They stood motionless, shoulder to shoulder, both men staring down at Jimmy. He was dressed in a grey thermal shirt and blue jeans and the collar of the shirt was dotted with blood and the pants were frozen stiff and frosted with ice. His neck was streaked and stained with the blood Boyd had not been able to wash clean.

Help me get him out, Boyd said to his father. But his father didn't move. His face was slack and expressionless and he just stared at his son as if he were staring down at a ghost.

Boyd watched his father for a long moment then he turned for the door and walked out to the truck. When he came back in his father hadn't moved. Boyd dropped the tarpaulin onto the wooden floor and it made a dull thud that failed to gain his father's attention.

What happened? his father said, finally, his voice cracked and strained in the emptiness of the cabin.

He shot himself, Boyd said. The wound's on the other side of his head. Just behind his eye.

Was it mine? his father asked.

The gun?

Yeah.

Yeah, it was yours.

I gave him that gun on his tenth birthday.

I know, Boyd said. I suspect that's why he used it.

He's a grown man Boyd why'd he do this?

He was only twenty daddy.

His father moved forward, placing his outspread palms on the lip of the ice chest. He stared down at his son and shook his head as if Jimmy had asked a question and the answer was no. He's wearing a long sleeve shirt.

We have to bury him, Boyd said.

How long has he been like this?

Since February.

Shit Boyd. It's damn near the end of July.

Like I said, he's been out here a while.

What, you just found him dead and decided to freeze him?

Boyd shrugged. We need to get a move on. It's fixing to rain real soon, he said.

His father cut him off. Answer me, son.

Boyd let go of the tarpaulin and it came to rest between his father and himself as if it was some sort of barrier that had to be breached before they could move on.

I didn't want our family going through any more shit. After you killed that man and got locked up Mama started running around, making a damn fool out of herself and our family. And when she remarried, well, Jimmy couldn't take it, he just caved in. Guess all the weight of watching you sit in prison and Mama moving on like none us ever existed just crushed him.

His father stood silently, listening, his arms folded across his chest.

Our family was falling apart.

Didn't anybody ask where he was?

Folks just figured he had moved after Mama had left. The whole county knew he was pissed off at her.

His father breathed heavily. Did he leave a note?

Boyd shook his head no. When he discovered Jimmy's body Boyd didn't find a note nor did he expect Jimmy to leave one for that matter. He preferred his actions and his expressions to speak for him. You going to help me or not?

They spread the tarpaulin out a few feet from the ice chest and it took both men and all their natural strength to free Jimmy's body from the frozen ice. Boyd had to run out to his truck for a shovel so that he could chip away the life size chunk of ice that held Jimmy captive. His father took Jimmy by the shoulders while Boyd grabbed him by his ankles and his body was so cold it took them several attempts before they heaved his dead body out of the ice chest and onto the tarpaulin.

Jimmy was lying on his side and the single bullet hole in the space between his ear and eye looked like a birth mark or a scar from his youth. The two men just stared down at him for a long moment before they wrapped his body in the tarpaulin and half carried half drug his body to the truck. They did all this without words or expression like they were two strangers sent to complete a job.

His father sat in the cab of the truck and smoked while Boyd tied Jimmy's body down with bungee cords and when he finished he righted himself and looked over to the stand of sugar maples and the western sky. He watched the lightning bloom then douse everything in intense flashes of light.

Back some time long before Boyd and Jimmy were born their great grandparents had created a small burial ground. It was a plot of land no bigger than that what a small house would consume and it was tucked away back in the woods behind the house Boyd and Jimmy had grown up in.

It was raining as Boyd parked the truck in the old driveway where his father once parked his pickup truck long ago, back when Boyd's family all lived together, back when at least the idea of happiness had been around.

This isn't right, Boyd, his father said. It was the first time either of them had spoken since removing Jimmy's body from the ice chest and the sound of his father's voice sounded strange and broken.

Never said it was.

So you just want to bury him? Dig a hole and toss Jimmy in there?

Boyd nodded. He deserves this at least.

He had been waiting to do this since he had found Jimmy's body but he wanted his father there too. Because he thought by making his father bury his own son it would make everything right. Like he would find justice in watching his father slumped over a shovel digging the grave for Jimmy.

I can't drive the truck back there, Boyd said. Looks like a jungle.

It was raining harder now and the sound of the rain on the hood of the truck muted out Boyd's inner thoughts. His father turned in the bench set and lowered his head as if to see better through the rain. Maybe we could find a wheelbarrow.

Boyd shook his head no. We'll have to carry him. C'mon let's go.

They trudged through the rain and the summer dust was rapidly transforming into mud the two men slipped on. They used the truck for balance and Boyd lowered the tailgate and undid the bungee cords from the eye hooks on the truck. They pulled on the tarpaulin until it was on the edge of the tailgate and the top of Jimmy's head showed through a section of the tarpaulin and his father pulled it taut to cover it back up.

They looked at each other, holding one another's gaze for a moment, rain running out of their hair and into their eyes, their boots already filled with water.

You ready? Boyd asked.

His father drew in a painful breath and nodded and they began the task of carrying Jimmy's body to the family graveyard.

The wind was blowing hard in all directions and the rain came at them slantwise as a result, stinging their faces. Thunder shook the ground and lightning cracked repeatedly as if signaling to the dead the arrival of another.

There were a total of seven headstones protruding from the earth and they stood tall in the oncoming wind like a line of soldiers awaiting battle. They dropped Jimmy's body onto the ground out of fatigue and both men shuddered as Jimmy hit the dirt and mud.

I'll go back for the shovels, Boyd said.

His father wiped away the rainwater from his brow and nodded.

Boyd returned to find his father sitting next to Jimmy's body, his head titled down and his hands knotted around the base of his skull. He was talking quietly to Jimmy as if Jimmy were still alive, as if Jimmy might just sit up and join the conversation. Boyd leaned against the wet bark of a white oak tree. He strained to listen to his father through the wind and rain.

I'm so sorry, son, his father said to Jimmy. I'm so goddamn sorry for all of this. I never meant for things to turn out like this. You were a good kid, Jimmy. You deserved a lot better than what you got. All I ever wanted was the best for you and Boyd. That's all I ever wanted, his father said before his voice trailed off to silence and all they were left with was the sound of the rain and the trees rattling in the wind.

They dug a hole no deeper than four feet because the rain continued to wash the mud back into hole and as soon as his father had flung it all out the hole was no sooner refilled with mud and rainwater.

This'll have to do, Boyd said.

His father shook his head. Can't. Damn dogs and coyotes will sniff him out and eat on him, Boyd.

The rain. It's not letting up. We're fighting a losing battle. Let's just get Jimmy in there and cover this thing up the best we can.

His father was knee deep in the hole and his hands were caked with mud and his face was streaked black with it. He looked tired, like he was digging the hole for himself, like he was ready to climb in.

They laid Jimmy's body to rest gently and before Boyd tossed the mud and dirt back into the hole his father peeled back a section of the tarpaulin and pressed his fingers against a part Jimmy's flesh and whispered something to Jimmy only Jimmy could hear then he climbed out of the hole and headed back to the truck.

Boyd refilled the hole with dirt and mud and with his hands he smoothed the mound out the best he could then he carried over armfuls of wet, soggy leaves and dropped them onto the freshly dug grave. Next he laid the wreath of wet flowers near where Jimmy's head probably was and he told Jimmy he'd be back real soon with a granite headstone.

At a motel parking lot they sat in the idling truck wet and muddy. The rain was more of a soft mist and the thunderheads from earlier had been escorted by the wind further east. Boyd looked over at his father.

Here. He pushed a brown envelope across the bench seat.

What's this?

Open it.

His father slid his finger under the seal and stared down at its contents.

Thank you Boyd. I appreciate it. Really. But I can't.

The key is for room 218, Boyd said. Up those steps over there.

His father pulled from the envelope two crisp hundred dollar bills and the single room key on a bronze key ring.

And the money? What's this for?

It's all I can afford. I know it's not a lot, but I figured it may get you started.

I can't, Boyd. Not after all I've done to you.

Boyd shook his head and dropped his eyes and stared down at the small puddles of murky brown water that had pooled on the floorboard of the truck.

You can't hate me more than I hate myself, his father said.

I never said I did.

It's in your eyes, son.

Boyd looked out the window at the oncoming night. A few stars sparkled to the west.

Thank you, his father said. For all this. For letting me say goodbye to Jimmy.

Boyd didn't turn around.

You got a job lined up, Boyd said.

No.

Heard the truck plant's hiring.

I'm too old for manual labor.

Parole officer will be on you for one.

His father nodded. Yeah, I know. Figure I might just leave though. Head somewhere new. Start over. Take this money and hop a bus.

They'll find you. You know that, yeah?

His father chewed his bottom lip. They ain't coming for me. They'll forget about me by tomorrow, Boyd.

His father opened the truck door and stepped down onto the gravel.

Where you going? Boyd asked, not really wanting to know but a part of him deep inside did and that was enough for Boyd.

His father shrugged. I'll write you when I get there. How's that?

Boyd nodded.

Give the little one a hug for me, okay? his father said and guided the door with the open palm of his hand shut until it clicked, so that what Boyd told him next only Boyd heard. For the rest of his life.

DREW MCCOY IS A WRITER LIVING IN KENTUCKY. HE'S BEEN PUBLISHED IN NUMEROUS PUBLICATIONS AND HIS PLAY, "THE LONG WAY HOME" WAS A 2007 HEIDMAN AWARD FINALIST. HIS SHORT STORY, "HOW TO BE LOVED" IS CURRENTLY BEING ADAPTED INTO A SHORT FILM BY T5G PRODUCTIONS AND SHOULD HIT THE SHORT FILM CIRCUIT LATER THIS YEAR. CURRENTLY HE'S WRITING A HISTORICAL NOVEL SET IN 1937.

HE CAN BE REACHED AT WWW.DREWMCCOY.COM.

THE ACCIDENT

BY CONNOR DE BRULER

Hear the soft whimpers of the maimed animal in the night. Open the truck door and feel rain. The water is high on the road, as if it were a shallow creek. Step out into darkness and see the dog lying in the median on it's side. It howls in agony. There was nothing that could have been done, and the dog is lucky to even be alive. It raced out of the woods and was caught in the head lights. If the breaks had been slammed, the vehicle would have hydroplaned into the foliage, and the dog would be looking down at you in the steaming wreckage.

Check for cars at both sides. The only sound is of rain. The only light is from your vehicle. Touch the dog. It makes no noise. Try to pick it up. It whimpers slightly, yet seems to have no qualms against it. You place the dog into the back of your Ford and drive off, windshield wipers screeching along like straight razors to liquid stubble, into more darkness. You don't know where you are, or how far above or below the state border you've driven. You don't know what road you're on. You don't know where the nearest town is, and you don't know what to do with an injured Labrador in the back seat. For the next thirty-minutes the world is an endless road coupled with darkness and trees. The obscurity is overwhelming. The Labrador hoists itself up and attempts to look out the rear window. You try to keep it from hurting itself, but you realize, as it starts barking and whimpering, that it sees something, something in the distance shrouded by the forest. Did you see anything? Perhaps not, the road like this at night is home to many fleeting images that grapple their onlookers and then vanishing before any immediate recognition. They vanish into the obscurity, the nothingness, the collective subconscious. But perhaps you did see something, something that had not been placed there by your brain scrambling to interpret the darkness, scrambling to offset the sensory deprivation. Perhaps a silhouette was perched onto a tree branch, and in silence observed your vehicle making it's way down the long winding road.

The dog is not bleeding, so you have time, but you can't take it with you into the Smoky Mountains. You need to drop it off somewhere.

Up the road there is light. Houses begin to materialize; shops. You stop at a small convenience store. It looks as though it has been abandoned, yet the open sign and piercing florescent light says otherwise. You are still in the middle of nowhere. Exit the vehicle and walk inside. The dog scratches on the door and whimpers as you enter. See the old, hunched back man make his way from a chair near the drink cooler to the stool behind the cash box, across the creaking, wooden floor.

"How are you?" he says.

"Well, I don't know just yet."

"It's quite late to be thinking about that ain't it?" he asks.

Take out a bottle of water from the cooler, and a small tin cup from the shelves. Place them on the counter and ask, "I got an injured dog in the back of my truck. Is there anywhere I can take it, like a clinic or a veterinarian?"

He strokes his beard.

"Well, if you take that first right up the road here, and you head up for about half a mile there's a house in a clearing. It belongs to Mr. Townsend. He used to be a practicing doctor. Other than that, it's five miles to the next town. They have a clinic, but not an animal doctor."

"I see. Thank you."

Pay for your things.

"What happened to your dog?"

"It's not mine. I found it on the road."

"Does it have a collar on it?"

"No, no collar."

"How badly is it hurt?"

"There's no blood or anything sticking out of it. I'm pretty sure it's ribs are broken though. It looks like it's been hit." you say. You don't want to tell him it's your fault.

"Yeah, your best bet it to drive up to Doc. Townsend. He'll help you out."

"I suppose I don't have an other choice."

Walk outside. The dog is still crying. Open the back side door. It smells like wet for and piss. The dog has relieved itself on the back seat. Place the tin near it's face where it rests, and pour the water. It drinks quickly as though it has been running for miles. When it finishes the tin pour the rest of the cold bottle of the water inside, and shut the door.

Take the first right, and proceed up the road. The rain lessens. The dog begins to bark at the trees lining the road outside the vehicle. You can see nothing. There is only darkness.

"What the hell are you barking at?"

It is at this moment you begin to wonder just why the collarless Labrador came racing out of the foliage and into your headlights. The dog ran from the woods at full speed. You slowed down as much as possible, but knew you would hit it. Why was it running? Why would it have been running so fast? And now, why was it always barking at the woods?

Pay closer attention to road. Try not to look at the woods on either side of you. Try not to stare into the endless vacuum. You know what happens if you stare into those chasms. They envelop you. They become you, and you become a part of them. You become a part of nothing. The thin stretch of asphalt is your world.

The dog continues to bark.

"Shut up!"

You speed past a clearing in the foliage. In it, the blackened silhouette of a roof top is visible against the starry night opening itself up after the rain. Pull a U-turn and cautiously drive up the gravel road toward the house. You can now see that one of the windows glows a dim, orange. It's a good sign. Walk up the wooden steps to the front door in the light drizzle. Ring the door bell. No one answers. You think for a moment. Leave the dog here on porch. No, you can't do that. What's the right thing to do? Take the dog to the next town. No, you'd just have to deal with the others, the other people.

Run, you think. That's what you do best. You're a runner. You move from town to town. You don't like people. You figure they don't like you much either.

Ring the door bell. Hear nothing.

Forget it, you think.

Turn around to leave, then hear the distant sound of footsteps coming from inside. You hear something else from another direction. It sounds like scratching. Before you can comprehend it the door cracks open. You see a silhouetted face in the narrow opening.

"Do you know what time it is?"

"Yes sir, I'm aware of the inconvenience. It's just that I..."

"It's just that you what?"

"Well, it's an odd situation really."

"I'll say."

"I have a wounded dog I picked up off the road, and there aren't any veterinarians around. The gentlemen from the convenience store up the road said that you..."

"You're mistaken. I can't help you."

"I don't know what to do with an injured dog." you say.

"And you think I do?"

"Weren't you a doctor?"

"I was an eye doctor." he says. "So, unless that dog needs a pair of glasses I can't help you."

He slams the door shut.

Move down to the truck and hear the dog whimpering again. You have no choice. It's time to give up with your attempts of passing the buck. Take the dog with you to Tennessee.

As you close in on the truck in the dim light, you notice a striking difference in the appearance of your car. It seems to be glowing, giving of a silver aura of some sort. Draw nearer and see that it is only reflecting the waxing gibbous moonlight. See that the ubiquitous white paint of the truck has been peeled away by something. Something was scratching at the rear door, scrapping the paint away. Something was trying to get inside. Visions of a mammalian predator enter your mind; some kind of dangerous stalker smelling the wounded canine.

Cautiously get back into the car and drive off as fast as you can. The dog is still whimpering in the back as if it's afraid of something. You don't dare look back. However, you do take a brief glance in your rearview mirror. You see nothing.

After a full night of driving, you roll into a secluded Appalachian town. It's name is unremarkable, and therefore you forget the minute you read the welcome sign. You have bags under your eyes, and feel like collapsing onto the steering wheel and ultimately driving into one of the oak trees the proliferate the edge of the road here. You don't hear the dog's whimpers and assume that it has died.

Park outside a tiny outfitting firm, and walk in. The young boy in hiking gear behind the cash register greats you.

"Hello."

"Is there an animal hospital in this town?"

"Yes, the Veterinary clinic also serves as an animal hospital."

"Where is it?" you ask, exasperated.

"You simply go straight down the road hear until all you see are cow pastures, and take a right on Hopkins. It stands alone, and should be easy to spot."

Walk out without thanking him. Drive. Drive where he told you to drive. The road is no longer a road, rather a thin strip of gray sandpaper eating away at your senses. The white dividing lines materialize into doves and fly away. You're having a hard time not believing your own hallucinations from sleep deprivation. You begin to wonder: Just what did you actually experience last night? Are there still scratch marks on your truck left by some unknown force you never saw, or was that also a hallucination? What did you see in the forest? Did you see anything? Perhaps you did. The dog is still completely silent. You dare not look at it though.

You park now, in what you hope is an Animal Hospital. Exit the vehicle, and trek across the black top. The sky is gray, and promising rain. Enter through the sliding glass doors, and make your way to the reception desk. They can tell you are not well, and worry that you are drunk.

"Can I help you?"

"Yeah, I hit a dog last night, and I need..." You pause. "I've been looking for a Vet all night, and...." Take a breath. Before you can continue, the receptionist places a warm hand on yours and says, "It's okay. It's not your fault, and we won't hold it against you. Now, what's wrong with the dog?"

You say, "Well, you see, that's the problem. I think it's dead now, but I can't go back out there."

"What do you mean?"

"It's in the back of my truck. I just can't bring myself to check and see if it's still alive."

"Here's what I want you to do. I want you to go have a seat, and I'll get Dr. Stevenson to take a look okay?"

"Okay."

Take your seat. Sit sideways preparing for rest. A man with a white coat walks into the waiting room.

"It's the white truck?"

"Yes sir."

He walks outside.

When he walks back inside his face is completely expressionless. He doesn't look at you. He goes straight over to the reception desk, and pulls out a pen and a notepad. Quickly scribbling the note, he hands it to the receptionist. It reads, "Don't panic. Calmly call the police. There's a dead women in the back of his truck."

Connor de Bruler grew up in Greenville, South Carolina and has lived in Indianapolis, and Nuremburg, Germany. He has been previously published in Bending Spoons Literary Journal, Fictional Publications, and Glossolalia Magazine.

"THE LAST CONFESSION"
BY PATRICK BRIAN MILLER

Father Jonathan Brady snapped away from his doleful thoughts as the rusted, red Bronco jolted over another jagged pothole on the dirt road leading towards his punishment. The noxious fumes of dust-laced oil saturated the steamy, unforgiving air that blasted across him through the cracked window. Behind them, a thick trail of dust kicked high into the air, blurring any thought of his retreat. Before them lay a long, twisted trail of eroded dirt and endless pines baking in the mid-August noon.

The sweat-soaked face of his driver, Nick Broder, had become more and more anxious as they came closer to the small town of Phoenix, their destination. Nick's inane, constant chatter had become slowly sporadic and then blessfully buried underneath a gritty resolve to arrive at—and then quickly leave—the dreaded place.

Brady recalled again the ridiculous rumors and myths surrounding the isolated, abandoned town of Phoenix, empty of life save for the solitary priest whom Brady would soon replace. But despite the stories, the only fear that Phoenix aroused in him was a desperate recognition that his career was doomed. What had he done that would cause the Bishop to inflict this assignment upon him? Of course he hadn't connected well with the rural, simple-minded parishioners who had made up his first congregation. But then why not reassign him back up North, or even perhaps overseas, where he could make a real difference?

Brady's dream had always been to work in the Vatican, but instead he had been assigned to a small, country parish in the deep South. He had always tried to hide his disdain and disappointment from his congregation, but their beady eyes must have seen through his thin mask of cordiality. They had answered his inner thoughts by complaining to the Bishop, he was sure. And his punishment: an assignment to this awful place that time had long since passed over.

Phoenix had once been a thriving cotton town in antebellum days. As the county seat before the War, it had once boasted its prosperity with impressive, graceful mansions and a picturesque town square dominated by a stately courthouse. But Yankee raiders had burned much of the town to the ground. Undaunted, the town had quickly resurrected itself around a new, shiny red brick cotton mill that prospered for twenty wonderful years. However, a fated flash of lightning had burned it to the ground as well, leaving only a broken, brick skeleton. A single tower was left standing to guard the tomb of rubble.

Ten years after the fire, a terrible flood had washed away the remnant of inhabitants still determined to live in this cursed abode. So, around the turn of the last century, Phoenix had begun its long, lonely existence as a ghost town, visited only through the courage of teens who had lost a dare from their peers.

Five years ago, the Church had sent Phoenix its first semi-permanent resident. The small church that had once served slaveowners and had barely lasted long enough to see segregation had been quietly reclaimed and rededicated by the Church. The purpose of this newly consecrated church was still a mystery, even to Brady. He could only hope that Father Kelso, its first pastor, might shed some light on the matter before he left Brady with only the company of his unsatisfied curiosity.

A sudden hiss of white smoke from underneath the hood brought Brady back to his surroundings.

"Damn!" shouted Nick, with a sudden guilty glance at Brady. "Sorry, Father."

The Bronco slid to a halt on the dusty road, and Nick stepped out and lifted the hood. A flurry of smoke shot out, causing Nick to erupt into a few more involuntary curses. Brady stepped out, too, grateful to escape the sauna of the vehicle.

"How bad is it?" asked Brady reluctantly.

Nick sighed in frustration.

"The radiator is busted bad, Father. We're gonna need some help."

Brady glanced around at the Southern wilderness. He reached into his pants pocket and pulled out his cell phone.

"I'm not sure if this will work out here," confessed Brady, "but it's worth a try."

He squinted at the hazy glare on the small screen before twisting it into his shadow. With little hope, he pressed the power button, only to be greeted by a no-service signal.

Nick looked up and down the dirt road and came to a realization.

"It should work at the top of that hill a few miles back, Father," Nick offered.

Brady stared without enthusiasm at the still-spreading blanket of dust curling up behind them.

"Even if it works there," continued Nick, "it will take a couple of hours for someone to meet me. Phoenix is only about a mile or so down this road, if you want to walk it. As soon as I get help, I'll come back for Father Kelso."

"I suppose I'll manage," stated Brady, silently grateful to escape Nick's company. "Well, Nick, good luck then. I will see you later this afternoon." He handed Nick the phone and turned towards the last, long leg of his journey. He left his luggage in the Bronco for when Nick returned.

Brady launched into a steady, rhythmic stride, now eager to reach his destination. The automatic pattern somewhat eased the effect of the incredibly oppressive heat. The burning sun played strange tricks on his mind, and he felt himself becoming a part of the harsh, humid landscape instead of merely suffering within it, as if he were a wild animal that belonged in this intimidating environment. Cool shadows underneath tall pines beckoned to him on either side, but prickly walls of green thickets guarded the way. No matter; he was content now to walk forever along this road.

The road curved to the left about a quarter of a mile down, and he noticed a gradual change in the landscape. Lines of old wisteria began to cover the pines, and broken fence posts along with collapsed shacks began to dot the roadside. Instead of thick forests, overgrown fields and pastures began to slide into view. Finally, at the top of a small hill, he stopped to behold the town of Phoenix about a half-mile below.

Not much was left of the town, but he could distinctly make out the crumbling courthouse and ring of fallen buildings that had once made up what had probably been a beautiful town square. He searched for the renovated church and found its clean, white steeple in strange contrast with the rest of the ruins. He also spotted the lone tower of the burned out factory that had briefly saved the town from abandonment. Well, this was to be his home for the next year or so. He started again with an energetic pace fueled by a powerful sense of fate beckoning him on.

He had not taken three steps before a low, deep growl of thunder rolled across the land. Brady turned and saw the dark gray clouds gathering force a few miles away to the west. He didn't care if the storm caught him now—it would only offer relief from the dizzying heat.

As he made his way down the hill, he wondered again what purpose he was to serve here. He found it ironic that a town named "Phoenix" was to be perhaps the death of his career. Yet the Bishop had never quite stated that this assignment was a punishment for Brady's ineffective service. The Bishop had been brief and mysterious, saying only that Brady had been chosen and to follow any instructions from Father Kelso exactly. The Bishop's voice had been direct but not stern, and Brady still remembered the strange earnestness in the man's eyes.

The first lashes of thick raindrops began to pelt him as he made his way alongside the factory. He gazed up at the single tower appearing ominous in the onslaught, and he wondered how long it would stand before crumbling down like the rest of the town. He also wondered how much he could stand living in this desolate place alone. Brady had never been a very spiritual man, despite his profession. He had always been attracted to the scholarship of the Church and its rich cultural heritage rather than its emotional and spiritual aspects. But here in this place, he was as far away as possible from accessing the deep valleys of intellectualism that the Church had always provided him.

The power of the storm softened by the time that he had reached the church. The building was old but well-kept, even the manicured grass that surrounded its freshly-painted walls. Brady wiped a hand through his soaked hair and made his way up the wooden stairs. He knocked nervously on the thick, dark wooden doors and then cautiously stepped through.

Inside, the church was filled with a somber silence, broken only by the soft rustling of rain on the walls and windows. Tall, stained-glass windows sent cascades of color across the rich, thick, red velvet carpets, cushions, and dark wood pews. The gold surfaces surrounding the small altar glinted in the gentle candlelight, the only sign of life in the quiet space. The pews couldn't hold more than a hundred parishioners, yet their eerie emptiness seemed to fill the room with a thousand abandoned seats. Brady was grateful when a tall, thin figure draped in black robes emerged from a small door behind the altar.

"Father Brady," welcomed Father Kelso in a pleasant tone that filled the room with warmth. "I was wondering when you would make it here. Where is Nick?"

"I'm afraid that we had car trouble, Father Kelso," replied Brady. "Nick had to walk a few miles to get help. I walked here ahead of him."

Kelso squinted his blue eyes in the dim light and frowned, sending a ripple of creases across his old face.

"Why, you're soaking, Father Brady. Come with me, and I'll lend you some dry clothes."

"Thank you, Father," answered Brady politely. He followed the old man back through the door to a small, one-room rectory. Kelso gave him a towel and a clean set of clothes before returning to the main room. In a few minutes, Brady returned also, eager to have his questions answered at last.

Brady found Kelso gazing wistfully around the small church. He was surprised when the old man turned with tears in his eyes. Brady assumed that he was relieved to be finally leaving this lonely place.

"So, Father Kelso," began Brady with a sarcastic grin, "what did you do to be sentenced to this place?"

Kelso regarded him with a strange, intense glimmer of anticipation.

"I was chosen, Father Brady, just as you were. You will soon find that serving here is not a sentence but rather a special privilege."

"Forgive me, Father, but I can not see what privilege there could be in this place, other than for a monastic."

"No, you will not see," agreed Kelso, "but you will understand."

Brady held up his hands to emphasize the emptiness of the church.

"What are my duties here, Father Kelso?"

"You will have but one duty here, Father Brady. At three-thirty in the afternoon each day, you will hear confession."

"Confession?" laughed Brady in amazement. "I don't understand."

"But you will," assured Kelso with conviction. "At the designated time, you must enter the confessional. Do not leave it until the confession is fully heard. There will be a screen between you and the confessor; you cannot breach that wall of anonymity. Beyond that duty, your time is free." Kelso sensed Brady's frustration and placed a firm hand on his shoulder. "I did not understand at first, either," he admitted. "But soon, all will be clear. I must leave now, but I wish you the best of luck. Once a week, on Saturday afternoon, Nick will come with groceries and supplies. Let him know of anything you need, and he will bring it the next week. God bless you, Father Brady."

Without another word, Kelso walked out of the church. Brady followed him outside in stunned confusion, but the old man did not turn around. Brady watched him walk through the rain until he disappeared over the hill above the town.

Brady stood outside for at least a half an hour, pondering what the old man had told him. When the rain finally stopped, he glanced at his watch and frowned: 3:25.

Brady waited and watched for the next five minutes. He wondered if anyone would show up, and if they didn't, should he still enter the confessional? When the time had elapsed, he decided to fulfill his duty, on the off chance that somehow he was being watched. After all, such an occurrence couldn't be stranger than being sent here in the first place. He walked back into the church and listened to his own steps creak into the old floor beneath the carpet. He entered the small confessional just to the side of the main door and sat down on the hard, wooden bench. He pulled the curtain closed and waited in anticipation. The confessional was dark, and he could just make out the thick screen that separated his side from the other. He wondered how long he should wait if no one appeared.

But less than a minute later, he heard the heavy doors of the church open and a set of steps creaked around to the confessional. He heard the other curtain being pulled aside and closed, followed by the sound of a person sitting down.

"Bless me, Father, for I have sinned," panted the strained voice of a man.

"I am here," announced Brady, surprised and intrigued. "How long has it been since your last confession?"

"I don't know," admitted the man, sounding very distracted, almost confused. "I have two sins to confess."

"Go on," encouraged Brady, wondering what sin could cause this man to travel so far to confess.

"Last Saturday night, my wife and I attended a party," began the man. "She, Beth, asked me not to drink too much, but I didn't listen. She was drinking too, and I was supposed to drive us home."

Brady's mind cringed, for he could already guess where this confession might lead. He was used to hearing petty confessions of greed, jealously, lust, and anger, but few carried severe consequences. Already, the pain in the man's voice betrayed the horrific crime that he had committed.

"Remember, my son, all sins are forgivable in the eyes of the Lord," stated Brady.

"But I couldn't forgive myself, Father," whispered the man sorrowfully. "I had a wreck on the way home; my Beth died," he sobbed. "My beautiful Beth."

The unbearable pain in the man's voice singed Brady with pity and compassion. Brady had never felt comfortable with emotion, and dealing with this man's inner torture was almost too much to stand. He felt a sudden, powerful impulse to run from the confessional rather than help this poor soul to overcome such incredible grief. After all, what could he, even as a priest, say that could possibly help this stricken man to overcome self-guilt when the man was, irrevocably, guilty? This man would never live another day without remembering his crime.

"My son, I would be lying if I told you that there is some way to take away your pain. But perhaps, with God's love and forgiveness, your pain can be softened. Life is a precious gift, and each day of your life now is an opportunity to please the Lord."

"It is too late for me, Father," moaned the man. "I couldn't bear to live without Beth. Every second was torture for me."

"It is never too late for forgiveness, my son," countered Brady, summoning all of the confidence he could muster. He felt sweat beginning to pour out from his forehead. "Your life can still be used to bless the Lord."

"No, it can't," lamented the man. "For that is my second sin, Father. The day after my Beth was killed, I took my own life."

Brady's mournful eyes hardened. He immediately bolted up, tore through the curtain and ripped open the other side to reveal . . . emptiness. He scanned the confessional for some hidden speaker but found only solid wood. He stepped inside to examine the walls more closely, but he was filled with a harsh chilliness. He gasped at the coldness he felt inside and stepped back out reflexively.

Brady stood, panting in confusion, for he knew that no one could have escaped that fast. He also knew that there was no speaker. Or perhaps the speaker was inside the screen. He reached his arm slowly back into the confessional, but the same severe cold immediately shivered up his skin. He pulled his arm out and noticed chill bumps rising before his eyes. Brady stepped away from the confessional now and stared at the empty seat with horror. He could still sense the presence of the man, despite what his eyes were telling his brain.

"No," he whispered to himself, unable to believe. No, this could not be his duty. But he knew that it was. Now, he understood.

Brady's body shook as he reentered his side of the confessional. With trembling hands, he closed the curtain again and sat. For the first time that day, he prayed. He asked for courage, for guidance, for anything that could get him through the next terrible minute of his life. Then he spoke again.

"I am here," he began.

"It is so dark," moaned the voice. "So empty."

"You are a child of God," Brady reminded him firmly. "You were sent here for forgiveness, and forgiveness you shall receive. Are you sorry for your sins?"

"Yes," whispered the voice.

"Then the Lord forgives you, my son."

"What of my penance, Father?" asked the voice.

Brady's eyes welled with stinging tears as he placed his hands on the screen.

"You have already suffered your penance, my son. Go in peace; the Lord will light your way."

"Thank you, Father," whispered the voice. Brady heard him gasp in amazement. "Father, I see the light! I see it!"

"Follow the light, my son," instructed Brady, wiping his tears away. "Follow the light."

PATRICK BRIAN MILLER

MONTGOMERY, ALABAMA

TO LEARN MORE ABOUT THE REAL PLACES AND EVENTS
THAT INSPIRED THIS STORY, PLEASE VISIT MY
FACEBOOK.COM WEBSITE USING MY E-MAIL ADDRESS:
JYORR@AOL.COM

Cut Through Road
by Chris Deal

I met Lloyd in 1972. Was not long after my Daddy died. Momma said it was a heart attack that took him, that he was walking up to Pucket's store and died halfway there. He'd fell down on the side of Cut Through Road.

When I walked the road that they'd cut through a tobacco field I could always find a warm breeze blowing through, even then near the end of summer before they brought in the plants. I was walking along the same road, heading up towards Pucket's store when I was stopped by a couple of white men in a knocked up truck. They pulled up beside me and got out, a taller boy with bright red hair and a shorter, blond one. The blond one didn't have no shirt on and had a drawing on his arm of a naked lady. The tall boy had a knife and told me to give him my money.

I said I needed it for a biscuit. I walked up to Pucket's about once a day except for Sundays for a jelly biscuit and a Coke but that tall boy just told me to give him my money.

They came close and the blond one took my hand in his and twisted it up beyond my back and it hurt. The tall boy put that knife to my belly and said he weren't going to ask again.

About then a blue truck pulled up behind theirs and a man came out holding a baseball bat and he was yelling for them to get away from me and some words my Momma told me not to say. The blond one let go of me and the tall boy turned that knife to the man.

He had light brown hair cut short and he was strong looking, taller than that blond one but shorter than the redhead. He took that bat and swung at the knife and that tall boy his hand went limp and the knife went out into the tobacco field the road cut through and that boy started yelling when that bat hit the blond boy on the jaw and he spat blood and went to the ground. The tall boy went to turn and run but that bat got him in the side and he went to his knees and the bat got him on the head and he was quiet and not yelling no more.

You alright, the brown haired man asked.

I said yes, sir.

You don't have to call me sir, he said.

My Daddy always said to say sir, I said, and he said your Daddy sounds like a smart man.

Yes, sir, he was, I said.

He asked my name and I told him and he said hello, Frank, I'm Lloyd.

I guess by then he seen how I was. He asked me if I knew how to keep a secret and I said it was the least I could do. He said something about those boy's plates, how it didn't look like no one around there would miss them, not around here. We stood there a bit, him breathing heavy like my Daddy used to do and wiping his forehead with his hand and me not knowing what to do. I was hot and hungry and wanted to go get a biscuit and go home to Momma.

Where were you going, he finally asked. I told him Pucket's store and he thought on it and reached to his back pocket for his wallet. He pulled out a couple of bills, bigger one's than I'd seen. I get checks from the government but my Momma always took care of those and would give me money for Pucket's but never bills as big as those.

I was heading that way myself he said. If you could do me kindly and pick me up a loaf of bread and some eggs you could keep what's left. I'll take care of those two and give you a ride home.

I said that sounded about right.

I walked on like I'd been only with more money, thinking over and over to myself bread and eggs, bread and eggs. At Pucket's, the owner Ronnie helped me out like usual, not saying nothing about the big bills I handed him. He just slipped one back over the counter to me and pressed a couple of buttons on the register and changed the big bill out for smaller ones and handed them to me and wished me a good day. Ronnie was always a good fellow, especially for a white man. He and my Daddy were always good friends, so I always liked him. I said thank you, sir and got the bag and my coke and left. Outside I nodded hello to a white man who was getting gas for his shinny car and he said nothing back as I started for home.

Around when I got to where those boys had stopped me I saw their truck was gone, as were they. I kept on walking when the blue truck pulled up beside me. Hey, Frank he called from the open window. He asked if I wanted that ride and I told him sure.

He leaned over and opened the door. I got my biscuit wrapped in grease paper from the bag and handed him the rest and got in. To me, it was a nice pickup but I'm sure few else would have thought it.

I pointed the short ways home and we talked for a bit about nothing much. He did not ask again if I could keep a secret and I did not ask if he'd done that before. My Momma had told me about the war and how a lot of boys had to hurt people over there and keep from being hurt themselves. He seemed to me different from the folk I knew. He reminded me a bit of my Granddaddy who'd been over in France during the second big war, the way their backs were straight always, the respectful manner they talked to everyone. I'd ask Lloyd sometime later about it and he thought a moment and told me about some of the things he'd done over there but not too much to scare me. I never was scared of him though.

He pulled up to the house my Granddaddy had built when he'd gotten home from France and I had about forgot about the money left over from what he'd given me. I knew he'd said to keep it but I didn't know if he really meant it. When I pulled it from my pocket he just waved it away and said a promise is a promise and that I deserved it. When he pulled away I thought it'd be the last I'd see of him.

Three days later I'd walked up to Pucket's for my jelly biscuit and a Coke. Sitting out front when I went to walk home were a couple of old white men and then that blue truck pulled up to the pumps and Lloyd came out and waved at me. One white man, a bald one called Tunny, turned to the other named Curt and said Curt do you know what's worst than a nigger?

Can't quite say I knows what, he responded.

A retarded nigger and they both laughed hard at it. My Momma told me never to listen to those who said things like that. They was worst off than me by a lot she'd say. I was about to walk home when I saw Lloyd walk over to them and lean down close to their faces and he whispered something and they went pale and when he stood up I thought I saw him put something shiny back into his pant's pocket.

Do we have an understanding he said and they nodded and he went in and paid for his gas and when he came back out they were still there, quiet and doing all they could to avoid looking me in the eyes. He asked if I wanted a ride and I said sure.

In his truck he asked I ever played checkers. My Daddy used to play with me and my brother when we were kids but not much since, I told him.

We should play some, then, he said. He drove back to his house, an old cabin a couple of miles from my home. It had electricity and water but not much else. The cabin had a kitchen and bedroom that were not separated and a bathroom. There was a table by the fireplace where he set up the checkerboard. Want to be red or black, he asked. I said, Red.

We played for a couple hours, him winning mostly but I had some good games. During the play we talked a little, getting to know each other as friends do. He told me about the war and I told him about what it was like growing up, the way I was. He went quiet when I asked him what he did. After a few minutes and he asked to be kinged, he said he stole things. I didn't ask anymore.

When he drove me home he said I like you and I thought that was funny. He said I reminded him of himself, only as a better person. After that he said he couldn't stay in town much longer. He had to take of things with his father. He asked if I liked his cabin and I said it was nice. If I wanted, he said, I could use it if I needed. He dropped me off at home and we said goodbye and that was the last I saw of him.

The next day I went up to Pucket's and went to pay and Ronnie said it was taken care of. I had a tab and anything I needed would be taken care of. Those two old white men, Tunny and Curt were there but they didn't say a thing to me.

Sometime later, my Momma went to bed one night and didn't get up in the morning. I called my brother Jimmy and he came down from the city and he took care of matters. He asked if I wanted to stay there in my Granddaddy's home but I knew I could not take care of it like my Momma and Daddy had.

Jimmy had done good for himself and had a family in the city and asked if I wanted to come live with them but I didn't want to intrude on their lives. I told him about the cabin and he and I went to look at it and he asked the landlord who said the place wasn't his. Someone named Cooper had paid for it and kept up on the taxes. He had a letter from the man for me. It was from Lloyd, saying the cabin was mine as long as I wanted it and to take good care of it. Jimmy helped me move in and he took care of my parent's home, not wanting it to leave the family.

The night I moved in it was cold and I wanted to start a fire. The tobacco was still up but it'd been getting cold at night. There were some old logs out back and I brought them in and put them in the fireplace but when I pushed them towards the back, three of the bricks fell out and behind them was a package wrapped in old newspaper sitting in the hole. I was close to tears when I opened it. Several stacks of old twenty-dollar bills with a note from Lloyd that said to use the money but not too much, as some folks were looking for it.

The cabin was further from Pucket's than I was able to walk, so I used a small bit of that money to buy a bicycle from a neighbor. I hadn't much need for it, as my Momma had Jimmy help set up a trust fund for me, using the money she'd saved from her own work and what I got from the government. I needed to pay some utilities but that was it. With the bicycle I started going to the library and about once a week or so Jimmy and his wife would bring me to their home for dinner. That tab Lloyd had gotten me for Pucket's was still good and for once in my life I was living on my own, something Momma had said she doubted I'd be able to do but I think I would manage directly.

I took that bicycle down to Pucket's about a year after Lloyd left and as I was drinking my Coke I heard Ronnie and some men talking. They found an old truck deep in the woods out on the outskirts of the town with a couple of skeletons in it. They figured those guys were two crooks who'd been riding through and had gotten drunk and crashed into a big tree the truck was wrapped around and that was the last I heard of those two. Ronnie rang me up and put my stuff on the tab and wished me a good day and I said thank you, sir.

Sometime after I bought that bicycle I got a knock on the door early one Saturday morning. There was a man in a nice suit there who said he was from the FBI and wanted to ask me a few questions. I asked him to come on in and offered him some tea but he said no, thank you. I asked him what I could help him with and he asked if I ever knew a fellow named Dan Cooper and I said honestly, I didn't.

He held up an old twenty dollar bill and asked where I got that from and I guess it was one of those I bought the bicycle with and told him someone I knew a while back gave it to me. The FBI man asked for his name. I told him Lloyd and he asked if I knew his last name and I told him I didn't. He asked when was the last time I saw this man and I said it's been a year or so. He thought on it and I guess he knew that was all he'd be able to get from someone like me.

As he left he handed me a slip of paper with his number on it if I knew anything about where he could find the man. I told him yes sir, I would and he nodded and when he left I threw that piece of paper in the trash. I knew exactly where Lloyd or whatever that man called him was. On that letter he'd left with the former landlord he'd put his address. I even wrote him and told him about the FBI man and he wrote back asking why I hadn't told the man anything. Said he expected to have been caught long back. When I wrote I told him that he was one of the few people who never called me nigger or retard or faggot and that he was my friend. When he wrote back all he said was thank you.

CHRIS DEAL WRITES FROM HUNTERSVILLE, NC. HE IS THE FICTION EDITOR FOR RED FEZ, AND HAS PUBLISHED SEVERAL PIECES OF POETRY.

MANY THANKS TO NANCY J, MY LOVE.

What's In The Box?

by Rondal Robinson

I once met these two guys on the road, Adam and Jaime. They were young, just out of high school, and were going to meet another friend, Gary, whose car had broken down on the other side of the county. They were in a small, two-door hatchback, so picking up passengers meant squeezing in. Adam didn't want to pick someone up in the middle of nowhere. But Jaime wouldn't allow him to pass someone up if they needed help. He was like that.

They were speeding down the back roads, listening to music, and talk was at a minimum. Adam was driving; I believe it was his car. Jaime had ADD, or something like that, and couldn't stand Adam's silence. Everything Jaime would say, Adam responded with something short, if anything at all. Then it started raining.

As a general rule, it's not the greatest idea to pick up hitchhikers when it's raining. It's also not a good idea to pick them up on a deserted back road. While I'm at it, it's not a good idea to pick up hitchhikers when it's dark out, either. More to the point, it's just not a good idea to pick up hitchhikers at all. But Jaime wouldn't allow him to pass someone up if they needed help. He was like that.

Adam slowed down when he saw a figure dressed in bright yellow up ahead. A man in a raincoat turned to face them, his right arm out, thumb up high. He had a cardboard box, flaps folded, under his left arm. Instantly, all those warnings from Adam's parents rushed through his head. He heard his dad tell him to never talk to strangers. He heard his mother tell him to never pick up hitchhikers. The car slowly drove past the hitchhiker.

Nothing could be made out about him. He may have had a beard; he may have not. He may have had long, dark hair; he may have not. He may have had dark eyes; he may have not. Adam was sure the hitchhiker's eyes followed them as they went by. In the split second the stare was broken, it returned in the rearview mirror as he kept driving. Adam felt Jaime's foot crossed over his on the brake, and Jaime's hands crossed over his on the wheel. Then the car came to a sudden stop, something Adam never would have done.

"I can't let you pass someone up if they need help," Jaime said. He was like that.

They stared at each other. Adam was sure they were making a mistake; Jaime was sure they were not. In a small county, everyone knows everyone, and they didn't know him. Just then, the hitchhiker stood next to the passenger side window. Adam's eyes got wide, but Jaime still turned to open the door.

He yanked on a lever on the side of his seat and slid it forward as far as he could. The hitchhiker bent down and entered the car head first. Jaime readjusted the seat and slammed the door. He turned to Adam and told him to drive, which he did.

Rain dripped off the hitchhiker. The cardboard box, flaps folded, was sitting on his lap. Adam wanted to look at him in his rearview mirror, but couldn't, for fear of being caught. The hitchhiker just sat back there, perfectly still, not moving, not breathing, and not making a single sound. Adam waited for Jaime to say something to the new passenger. He waited again. He waited some more. Finally, Adam broke the silence.

"So where ya goin'?"

"Just drive," the hitchhiker said in a scratchy voice.

This ended Adam's conversation. Jaime didn't seem alarmed. He liked everybody and never pegged anyone as bad. Adam, on the other hand, was cautious and suspicious. He kept looking at Jaime out of the corner of his eye, waiting for him to say something. Finally, Jaime got anxious.

"Bad weather out there."

The hitchhiker said nothing.

"Didn't see yer car anywhere."

The hitchhiker still said nothing.

"We almost didn't see ya."

"I'm wearing yellow," the hitchhiker finally spoke.

Adam didn't know what to say. Jaime began to laugh. He turned to look at Adam. The hitchhiker leaned forward. Adam laughed and took a quick glance in the rearview mirror and saw part of his face. He was unshaven and had thin lips. He was smiling, smirking really, enough to make Adam relax, perhaps a little too much. Then Adam asked the question.

"What's in the box?"

The hitchhiker got quiet, and then breathed slightly, a huff, exhaling in disgust. He leaned forward, his head about a foot behind Adam's. He waited a second, then responded, "that's none of your fucking business!"

The hitchhiker leaned back; Adam and Jamie looked at each other. It was becoming apparent on Jaime's face that picking up hitchhikers wasn't such a good idea. Still, they remained calm and quiet for the next minute. Then Jaime got worried.

"There's a gas station up here."

The hitchhiker said nothing.

"I'm sure they've got a phone."

The hitchhiker still said nothing.

"You can probly call somebody on it."

"That's what phones are used for," the hitchhiker finally spoke.

Adam didn't know what to say. Jaime began to laugh again. He turned to look at Adam. The hitchhiker leaned forward again. Adam smiled and took another quick glance in the rearview mirror and saw more of his face. He was smirking again, and his cheeks, what he could see of them, were ruddy and warm, enough to make

Adam relax again, perhaps a little too much. Then Adam asked the question, again.

"Come on, man, what's in the box?"

The hitchhiker got quiet, and then breathed a little heavier, a puff, exhaling in even more disgust. He leaned forward, his head about half a foot behind Adam's. He waited a few seconds, then responded, "that's none of your fucking business!"

The hitchhiker leaned back; Adam and Jaime looked at each other again. It was becoming more apparent on Jaime's face that picking up hitchhikers wasn't such a good idea. Still, they remained calm and quiet for the next few minutes. Then Jaime got nervous.

"You travel light."

The hitchhiker said nothing.

"Guess it's better on the road."

The hitchhiker still said nothing.

"Good idea ta carry all yer stuff in a box."

"This is my lunch," the hitchhiker finally spoke.

Adam didn't know what to say. Jaime didn't laugh. He didn't turn to look at Adam. The hitchhiker leaned forward some more. Adam frowned and took another quick glance in the rearview mirror and saw all of the hitchhiker's face. He was smirking again, his cheeks bloody, and his eyes were wild, much like a wolf, enough to make Adam unable to relax anymore, perhaps a little too much. Then Adam asked the question, once more.

"Seriously, what's in the box, man?"

The hitchhiker got quiet, and then breathed much heavier, he blew, exhaling nothing but disgust. He leaned forward, his head about an inch behind Adam's. He waited several seconds, then responded, "that's none of your fucking business!"

The hitchhiker leaned back; Adam and Jaime couldn't look at each other anymore. It was obvious on Jaime's face that picking up hitchhikers wasn't such a good idea. Still, they remained calm and quiet for the next fifteen minutes, their hearts racing, unsure of what to do. Jaime didn't want to talk anymore. Adam didn't want to look in the rearview mirror anymore. Then the hitchhiker spoke again.

"Up here!"

They looked up, and there sat an old, rusted station wagon, half in a ditch, hazard lights blinking, with road flares surrounding the car, but burned out from the intense rain. The hitchhiker's hand was between their heads, pointing at it. They knew it was Gary's car, but he was nowhere to be seen.

"I need to get something out of my vehicle," the hitchhiker finally spoke.

They came to a sudden stop, as did their hearts. Jaime yanked on a lever on the side of his seat and slid it forward as far as he could. The hitchhiker bent down and exited the car head first. Jaime readjusted the seat and slammed the door as the hitchhiker walked towards Gary's car. He turned to Adam and told him to drive, which he did.

The car sped off, standing still for a split second on the wet pavement, before passing the hitchhiker. Adam was sure the hitchhiker's eyes followed them as they went by. In the split second the stare was broken, it returned in the rearview mirror as he kept driving. The hitchhiker stared at them as they drove off. This time, nothing was going to stop him, not even Jaime, who normally wouldn't allow him to pass someone up if they needed help. But he wasn't like that anymore.

They didn't speak for the next hour, they just drove, lost on familiar roads that didn't seem so familiar anymore. Jaime sat emotionless; Adam seemed bothered the most. It wasn't the headlights in the rearview mirror that bothered him, it was something even worse. He didn't turn around, only pointed at it in the mirror. Jaime looked behind them, then turned back, looking straight ahead. Where the hitchhiker once sat, was the cardboard box, flaps folded. And as this tale moves toward it's end, you're probably asking yourself, "what's in the box?"

That's none of your fucking business!

Born the son of a steelworker and housewife,
Rondal Robinson eventually took up traveling
and writing across rural America, but got lost
somewhere along the highway. He occasionally
writes home.

Contact him at:

PO Box 176143

Ft. Mitchell, KY 41017

Or:

www.grimcounty.com

FRIENDSHIP

BY CYNDY EDWARDS LIVELY

"I'd kill him if I could get away with it," Everett said, smiling across the table at her best friend to take the sting out of the words.

The women sat in the café at Borders, having their weekly coffee klatch, sharing things they never even shared with their husbands. The bond between them went all the way back to that first day in Kindergarten when Mrs. Staley had sat them next to each other, going down the alphabet: E (no F or G in the class),then H. Everett and Hall. They used their husbands' names now, but that's how they still thought of each other – Everett and Hall.

They had gone separate ways during college, but had kept in touch: phone calls, letters, and summers spent together working as camp counselors. Then both of them returned home to Winston-Salem to get jobs and eventually marry and start families, never missing a beat in a friendship that had only grown closer over the years.

Hall returned her friend's smile. "Well, I wouldn't blame you. Nobody would."

Everett's only child, now twenty-two, lived up in the mountains of Ashe County with a man she had gotten involved with her senior year in high school. The young woman supported the two of them working as a cashier at a BP station after dropping out of Wake Forest University midway through her junior year. The guy had held various jobs during their five-year relationship, but none longer than a few months. He drank himself into a stupor most nights and was never out of bed before four in the afternoon. Over the two years they had been living together, the couple had moved from one poorly maintained rental to another, each filthier than the last. Everett suspected drugs, in addition to the alcohol, fueled their continuing slide.

No amount of yelling, pleading, or calm attempts at persuasion had made a dent in her daughter's self-destructive behavior. Occasional admissions that all was not well were followed immediately by a wall of denial. Her daughter insisted she was happy, living the life she wanted; her parents just didn't understand.

Hall's smile faded to a look of concern. "She didn't keep the appointment you made at the mental health clinic?"

Everett shook her head. "Cancelled out at the last minute."

"I thought she admitted she was depressed and agreed to get help."

"She did; but as usual, it didn't last. He managed to convince her that the whole thing was just another way for us to get them apart."

"What are you going to do?" Hall asked.

Everett shrugged. "What can I do?"

The friends met on the sidewalk and exchanged brief hugs before entering the café. It had been weeks since their last get-together. Family vacations and a trip to Ashe County by Everett, necessitated by her daughter's hospitalization for injuries in an automobile accident, had intervened.

"He's been charged with DUI," Everett said after they picked up their coffee order and took seats at a table by the window.

"Thank God, she's all right." Hall reached over to squeeze Everett's hand.

"The car's a total loss." It had been their high school graduation gift to their daughter. "I don't know how she's going to keep her job without transportation."

Everett gripped her cup in both hands and avoided her friend's gaze. "She refuses to leave him. We begged her to come home, get help for the depression and drinking, but she won't have any part of it." Everett looked up, tears blurring her vision. "I couldn't tell you this over the phone, but I'm sure he's abusing her. There were bruises I know weren't caused by the accident. At one point, she as good as admitted it; then she shut down, just like always."

"What are you going to do?" Hall said.

The look of horror on her friend's face jolted Everett from a fog of self-pity and denial. It was the question she had been asking herself since returning home from the mountains. "I'm going to kill him." This time she made no attempt to pass the words off as a joke.

It was a measure of the depth of their friendship that Hall only nodded in acknowledgement at the words. No protest that Everett didn't really mean it; that it was only the craziness of her fear talking.

Two months passed. Everett and Hall met weekly, exchanging family news, neither of them bringing up the threat. On a rainy December day as they sat at a corner table sipping coffee, Everett broke the silence. "I've figured out how to do it, but I'm going to need your help."

The café was crowded, and the noise of other conversations obscured her words. Elbows propped on the table, Everett leaned closer to her friend and outlined the plan.

"When?" was all Hall said.

"I'm driving up to Martinsville tomorrow to get the shotgun."

Virginia law allowed gun purchases without a waiting period or the necessity of supplying ID. There would be no record of the cash sale. It had been years since Everett had fired a shotgun, but her father had taught her to shoot skeet when she was a teenager. Once she had the gun in her hands, she would know how to use it.

"If you can get away next week," Everett said, "I'll make reservations at the spa. We'll say it's my Christmas present to you."

Now that she had come up with a plan, Everett was eager to get on with it. Otherwise, she was afraid she would lose her nerve and was determined not to let that happen. Her daughter's life depended on it.

Hall nodded agreement. They parted with solemn expressions and a hug that lasted a little longer than usual.

The air was crisp. Contrails from the planes flying in and out of Charlotte were all that marred the cloudless sky. Everett and Hall drove south on 77 and crossed the state line into South Carolina in a companionable silence. There was an unspoken agreement between them not to talk about the plan now that it was in motion, and other topics paled in comparison.

They drove into the Rock Hill Galleria parking lot an hour before the appointed time. Everett climbed from the car and watched her friend circle back to leave the lot. If all went well, they would meet up again by early afternoon.

Everett passed through Belk without a glance at the merchandise; she was in no mood to shop. The food court in the mall provided a selection of fast-food; she settled on a cookie and a carton of milk to calm her jitters.

At a quarter to ten, she pushed through the Sear's exit to scan the parking lot. It didn't take long for her to spot the thin, bearded man leaning against the battered, gray Honda Civic. Covering the distance in long, quick strides, she introduced herself by the name she had given over the phone. Fifteen minutes later, Everett had title to the car, and the man had eight hundred dollars in cash. The car wasn't much to look at, but it didn't need to be. Everett knelt and screwed the license plate from her daughter's car in place. They had never gotten around to turning it in after the accident.

The drive north to West Jefferson took a little over three hours; traffic in North Wilkesboro slowed her down. In spite of the chill breeze, she kept the windows cracked to dilute the odor of stale cigarette smoke that permeated the car. When she parked in the Wal-Mart lot, she headed straight to the pharmacy. Hall was waiting on the toothpaste aisle, a basket hanging from her arm loaded with items accumulated during her time in the store. She gave Everett a barely perceptible nod, strolled to the register, paid for the items in cash, and exited the door to the parking lot. Everett chose a stick of deodorant after browsing the extensive selection and did the same.

Hall's white Toyota blended in with similar cars on the lot, and it took Everett a while to find it. She slid into the passenger seat and smiled at her friend. "Everything went fine. The car's over by the main entrance, twelve spaces down the row. Let's get something to eat; I'm starved."

The western sky was a gorgeous display of pinks and violets when they arrived at the Grove Park Inn in Asheville to check in for the night. Hall drove into the deck under the Vanderbilt Wing rather than pull in at the main entrance. They wanted to come and go without using the valet parking. When they reached the front desk, Everett handed over her credit card for the room charges and confirmed their spa reservations for the following day. As she had requested, their room was in the old, historic part of the inn. They walked up the stairs rather than squeezing into the tiny elevator for the ride to the second floor.

After a quick shower and a change of clothes, the friends headed to the Great Hall Bar for a glass of wine. Fires burned in the enormous stone fireplaces, and no expense had been spared on the Christmas decorations. They sank into leather chairs and sipped chardonnay while they talked about what each of them still had left to do to prepare for the holiday.

The next morning, they checked in at the spa desk an hour before the first scheduled treatment. Hall headed for the locker room to change into her robe and slippers. Everett suddenly remembered that she had forgotten to leave her jewelry in the room safe. She gave Hall a brief wave, promising to join her after she had taken care of the errand. Her friend's smile was a little strained, but Everett was sure no one but she could tell.

Their spa treatments were carefully spaced throughout the day. Standing side-by-side, they would never be confused for one another, but they were similar physical types with the same coloring. The spa technicians would never know that Hall kept all of the appointments for the both of them.

Two and a half hours later, Everett cruised into West Jefferson after a single stop for a restroom break. When she made the turn off 221 onto Mt. Jefferson Road, she popped a Pepcid-AC into her mouth and washed it down with a swallow of water from the bottle she had brought with her from the room. Her stomach churned, and she wished she had eaten something more than half a blueberry muffin to soak up the coffee she had consumed at breakfast. At the time, she hadn't been able to get anything more past her lips.

It had been a restless night. Everett had listened to Hall toss and turn in the other bed. She had come close to offering to call it off if Hall was having second thoughts, but kept thinking of her daughter and how this was the only way out. He would end up killing her child one day if she didn't stop him.

Most of the vehicles in the Wal-Mart lot clustered around the main entrance. Everett chose a parking space near the pharmacy. She pulled a beat-up gym bag from the trunk, locked the car, and entered the building. Cruising the aisles, she made her way through the store to the main entrance without making a purchase.

It was almost a surprise to see the Honda where she had left it the day before. Minutes later she was headed up 194. The antacid had done its job, but her hands sweated so badly inside the latex gloves they felt like she had soaked in a tub for hours. Before taking the turnoff in Warrensville, Everett pulled onto a deserted side rode and stopped the car to exchange the license plate for one she had taken from a car in a parking lot on her trip up to Martinsville.

Her daughter still worked at the BP station. The couple had scrounged an old wreck of a car from somewhere. It didn't have a tag; and, of course, they didn't have insurance. Everett lived in terror of receiving a call about another car accident.

They lived in a trailer at the end of a dirt track that wound its way two miles north into the hills from the nearest paved road. Their closest neighbor was a dilapidated, clapboard house at the cutoff that didn't look occupied. The isolation increased Everett's fear for her daughter, but it also made the plan feasible.

The Honda jerked to a stop on the hard-packed earth in front of the trailer. Pulling a Braves cap low over her forehead, Everett stepped from the car and opened the trunk. No sign of life. Even the birds were quiet.

The thin painter's coverall she wore over her clothes wasn't much protection. In spite of the midday sun, Everett shivered. Stepping around trash bags piled at the entrance, she mounted the rickety, wooden steps and banged on the door with her fist. After several minutes, muffled curses and stomping feet signaled success.

She returned to stand by the trunk of the car and waited until the door swung open and he stood peering groggily out into the yard. His chest was bare, but he had pulled on a stained pair of jeans. His hair hung in greasy strings to his shoulders, and several days' worth of stubble covered his cheeks.

Everett froze. Just stood there staring at him, trying to figure out how her daughter had gotten mixed up with a lowlife like him in the first place.

"What the hell are you doing here?"

His question broke her trance. She unzipped the gym bag and pulled out the shotgun. One smooth movement and it was snug against her right shoulder and pointed at the center of his chest. She took two steps toward him, squeezed the trigger, pumped, and fired again. The way the shots shattered the stillness was almost as much of a shock as what they did to their target.

There was no need to draw closer to examine the results. She had never seen what a shotgun at close range did to a person and hoped to never again. For a few desperate moments, she was afraid she would vomit right there in the yard and was thankful her stomach was empty.

Stooping to retrieve the shell casing, she dumped it along with the shotgun into the gym bag, and slammed the trunk lid. Leaning on the car, she stumbled back to the open door and climbed into the driver's seat. Her hand shook so badly it was hard to turn the key in the ignition. After a few calming breaths, she managed to start the car and head back down the road.

The return trip to town was a void. One minute the car was turning onto 88 headed toward West Jefferson, and the next it had pulled to a stop in the parking lot of the Shell station. No one looked her way as she fumbled a quarter into the payphone and called the Ashe County sheriff's office reporting shots heard and giving the approximate location. Her daughter wasn't going to find him like that.

There weren't any free spots near the pharmacy when she reached the Wal-Mart lot, so she waited for a woman with three small kids in the car to pull out and took the space. Her vision dimmed and she grabbed the door handle to keep from falling on her face when she climbed from the car. Her chest squeezed down forcing quick, shallow breaths. It wasn't until her lips felt tingly and her fingers began to cramp up that she realized she was hyperventilating. Get a hold of yourself, she chided. You're almost home free.

Lifting the gym bag from the trunk, she took a quick look around. The cold kept everyone moving at a brisk pace; no one lingered in the parking lot longer than necessary. She slipped into the Toyota. The Braves cap, coverall, shoe covers, latex gloves, and the key from the Honda disappeared into a plastic garbage bag wedged under the front passenger seat. Her hands managed to grip the wheel, and her mind cleared enough to allow her to steer the car back to 221.

When the highway crossed the New River, Everett detoured onto a narrow road that ran parallel to the stream and stopped at a spot where trees crowded close to hug both banks. Her breathing finally settled into an easier rhythm as she watched the gym bag sink beneath the murky surface of the water. It took all her concentration to negotiate the curving, mountain route, and it wasn't until she reached Sparta that she was able to get her mind around the fact that she had really done it. The bastard was dead, and her daughter was safe.

Her hands were still shaky, but her stomach had stopped doing flip-flops and the hollow feeling was back. The sight of the Burger King on Main Street gave her the idea to solve two problems at once: hunger relief and waste disposal. She pulled around back to the drive-thru, tossed the garbage bag into the dumpster, and ordered a Whopper, fries and a small Coke.

The route from Sparta to 77 and then west on 40 to Asheville completed the circle without retracing her path. By the time Everett reached the parking deck at the Grove Park Inn, she was desperate for a toilet, but she hadn't wanted to stop anywhere along the way. The hallway was empty; no one saw her enter the room. When she finished in the bathroom, she kicked off her shoes and stretched out on the bed. It was important to stay hidden until Hall returned from the spa.

When the door swung open, the look on Hall's face told Everett how much of a strain the last two days had been for her friend.

"Did you do it?" Hall asked.

Everett nodded and rose to grasp Hall's hands. "She's safe now. I'll always be grateful. I couldn't have done it without your help."

Hall reached to hug Everett close. "You're my best friend. You know I wouldn't let you down."

CYNDY EDWARDS LIVELY IS A RETIRED PHYSICIAN
LIVING IN WINSTON-SALEM, NORTH CAROLINA. WHEN
SHE'S NOT WORKING ON HER FIRST NOVEL, SHE
ENJOYS HIKING IN THE BLUE RIDGE MOUNTAINS. SHE
MAY BE REACHED AT CELIVEL@TRIAD.RR.COM.

FINDERS KEEPERS
BY KATHLEEN GERARD

The day I met Georgette Whittamaker for lunch, the winds were whipping, the rains were pouring, and I was muddling through puddles as deep as canyons in the parking lot of the Freeze and Frizz luncheonette. As I hobbled up the stairs leading inside – balancing on my walker and a wobbly, wet old banister – Georgette was standing on the top step wearing a bright yellow rain slicker. She looked like a misplaced ray of sunshine on such a dreary day.

"Praise you, Lord Jesus," she proclaimed when she saw me coming, reaching her hands up toward the sky and catching raindrops on her palms.

This was my first clue that this lunch was going to be one of the biggest mistakes of my six decades of living.

"Georgette, please don't make a scene," I hollered, staggering up the stairs.

"Why, Marjery - the rains have broken free from Heaven like holy water from on high."

Just then there was a crack of thunder and a bolt of lightning that seemed to run sideways across the sky.

"God is so awesome, isn't He?" she shrieked. "Don't you just love Him?"

I swung my head, unimpressed, and pushed past Georgette into the Freeze and Frizz. I was hungry.

Inside, it was crowded and this being a Saturday, little kids were carrying on. Georgette and I ordered ourselves a couple of grilled cheese sandwiches, carried our plastic trays away from the counter and then squeezed our old, broken bodies into a flimsy booth. I pulled the paper off my straw, slipped it down into my root beer, and lifted the cup to take a sip. As I did, Georgette squeezed her eyes closed tight and flung her head back as if the muscles in her neck didn't have the strength to hold it no more. I gazed up, but only found a couple of rusty pipes and greasy tiles. When I looked back across the table and eyed the sight of her, I still couldn't figure out what was wrong. I reckoned she was a having herself a seizure or something.

"Georgette," I asked, leaning toward her. "Are you all right?"

Her meager voice soared loud and high. "Dear Lord!" she shouted as if she were actually trying to gain The Almighty's attention.

My body flinched. I jumped. My root beer spilled all over and my knees banged so hard into that Formica table, I thought my legs would bust right through the table top and make a mess of everything. Georgette not only got the attention of the Lord, but also every other patron in that eating establishment. It suddenly became hushed like a church.

"Let us pray, Dear Lord!" she declared again, pointing her palms to the ceiling and lifting her arms until they couldn't go any higher.

Oh, I was never so mortified. I kept my eyes and my fingers on my paper plate, revolving it around as if I wanted to turn back time and will myself away from this moment.

"Lord," she called. "Thank you for this meal we're about to receive . . ."

Georgette steepled her long, boney fingers together and bowed her head. She was so deep in prayer that I thought those grilled cheese sandwiches might just sprout wings, rise up from the table, and start fluttering all around.

". . . Thank you for the cook who prepared this lovely lunch. Thank you for my dear friend, Marjery, and the blessings of our friendship . . ."

When Georgette looked up at me and smiled, I half-heartedly curled the corners of my mouth. After all, folks were watching, and I didn't want to appear completely sacrilege.

" . . . Thank you for the green grass in the meadows and for allowing the cows to graze on such holy ground. Thank you for providing the milk and for giving us the curds, which separated from the whey, which produced the cheese for these glorious sandwiches..."

They didn't look so *glorious* to me. Why, the cheese that once looked all melted smooth now looked rubbery and hard.

"Shoot, Georgette," I said, finally cutting her off, "if you don't come up for air, we're gonna be thanking the Good Lord for the mold growing on these pretty soon."

Georgette frowned, all disappointed, but she did finally conclude with, "Amen."

"Amen!" I eagerly said that last part with her, as I flung out my napkin and slipped it onto my lap. The other patrons surrounding us soon followed my lead.

"May I please see the bill for lunch, Marjery?" Georgette asked.

"Forget it, Georgette. Don't you remember, this one's on me 'cos I broke your looking glass down at the beauty parlor last week?"

"I know. And your hospitality's mighty appreciated," she said. "But before I start eating, I always like to see what the good Lord has to say."

"I beg your pardon?"

"That receipt's a God-Gram."

"A what?"

"A God-Gram - a telegram from The Almighty," she announced. "If you look at any receipt close enough, you'll find God's message - like a Divinatory Horoscope. Now, if you would kindly fork it over. . . "

I stared at Georgette's palm reaching across the table. Begrudgingly, I lifted my root beer, peeled the soggy receipt off the table and slapped it into her open hand.

"Let's see" Georgette slid on her bifocals and eyed the slip of paper tape. It was as limp as a wet noodle. "It says our server was Matty – short for Matthew, I suppose –and our total was thirteen dollars and thirteen cents."

"Thirteen-thirteen. Why, that's a double-whammy of bad luck."

"Oh, Marjery, where's your faith?" Georgette pulled a pen from her pocketbook and scribbled *Matthew 13:13* on her napkin. "Why, believing in bad luck and superstition is just Satan's way of grabbing hold of you. Thirteen is a providential number. Why, Jesus and his twelve apostles made up the lucky thirteen."

"Oh, yeah. That Jesus was *real* lucky - dying on a damn tree," I told her. "And His dirty dozen disciples died even grimmer deaths . . ."

Georgette made a sour-looking face. She yanked out a big Bible from her purse.

The minute she started flipping the onion skin pages – some highlighted in bright, neon colors – I whined, "Oh, Georgette! You're not gonna start praying again, are you?"

"God speaks to us every minute of every day, Marjery. And the trick of living is to heed His message - His call," she told me, pointing a long finger upon her Good Book. "Why, everything we need to know about life is spelled out for us right here on these pages, in black and white."

I rolled my eyes as far back up into my head as they would go. "Well, while you're decoding your God-Gram. I'm gonna make myself a pit stop . . ." I ripped my napkin off my lap, threw it down on the table, and made a bee-line for the powder room.

So much for lunch!

I shuffled away. The wet, rubber soles of my orthopaedic shoes squeaked upon the oily-coated linoleum of the Freeze and Frizz. Once I was safely locked inside the stall of the latrine, I breathed a sigh of relief. But when I hung my head, I happened to spy a brown paper sack at the base of the bowl near the floor at my feet. I reached for it and when I crinkled open the bag, inside was a whole wad of hundred dollar bills. *Good God in Heaven!* A smile flexed the sagging muscles on my flabby face as I thumbed through bundles of green dollars. Why, there had to be as much as five thousand dollars in there.

I pressed the sack of money to my chest and stooped under the stall, searching for shoes and other signs of life. I was relieved to find myself all by my lonesome.

Thank you! Thank you, Lord! I sighed, hugging that paper sack and thinking of all the ways I could spend this fortune . . . *Maybe a plush, new La-Z-Boy recliner . . . Maybe a big screen HDTV . . . Hell, maybe even some liposuction on my thighs . . .* But in that small moment of conniving quiet, a pang of conscience started wiggling up inside of me like a free-floating burble of gas. But I quickly pushed all those feelings back down. After all, only a jack-ass fool would turn in this kind of money.

I tried to stuff that sack of dollars inside my brassiere. When that didn't work, I made straight for my support hose. But things in both areas were tight and busting out all over, so I had no choice but to cram that paper sack into my purse. I couldn't get the zipper to close, so I let it bulge out on top as I tucked my bloated pocketbook beneath my arm. Then I threw my shoulders back, flung my nose high in the air, and stood tall and proud – like any rich person should – and shuffled back to the table.

I didn't even have a chance to sit down, before Georgette started in again. "Well, do you wanna know what our God-Gram is for today?"

"Sure, why not," I said, squeezing my body back into the booth and looking over my shoulder to see if anyone could spy my sudden affluence.

Georgette buried her nose in her King James, cleared her throat, and read, "The book of Matthew. Verse 13, line 13, *The Purpose of Parables*: *'I use parables in talking to them because they look, but do not see, and they listen, but do not hear or understand. If they would just turn to me, says God, I would heal them . . .'* So what do you have to say about that, Marjery?"

I put a hand on my purse, brought it closer to my hip, and said, "Hallelujah!"

But just as those words escaped my lips, a fierce crack of thunder suddenly shook the skies, making the power inside the Freeze and Frizz wane. The lights flickered on and off and back again, and I heard all kinds of echoes ringing in my ears. I fiddled with my hearing aids. Most folks didn't even know that I wore them. I flicked the volume switch until suddenly, I heard a loud, manly voice – with a fierce, Southern drawl – say in one long breath, *'Two Buffalo Burger, one mega-fry, two sausage biscuit, double egg cream . . . Ten dollars and fifty-four cents.'*

"What in the hell was that?" I crowed, static filling my ears along with that same spewing Southern drawl. *'Would you like a sack with that or is it to stay?'*

I looked across the table at Georgette. Finally quiet, she was nibbling on her grilled cheese sandwich. I jiggled the plastic nodule thrust deep inside my ear. Once again, that Southern voice spewed fast and furious. This time, the words were running close together like an auctioneer who ground up way too many beans for his cup of Joe that morning.

'One Mile Long Texas Wiener, one barbeque squab, one rib, one ring, one Munchkin meal, large root beer, cherry coke, orange pop . . . Thirteen dollars and twenty-nine cents . . .'

"You can't hear *that?*" I asked Georgette. She shrugged her shoulders and swung her head as that man's voice kept being broadcast inside my head.

I shot my gaze all around that Freeze and Frizz, until I finally let my eyes rest upon the counter. There, I saw a very tall man standing at the ordering microphone - a man wearing this enormous, metallic and rhinestone belt buckle which spelled out the word *Jesus.* I watched his lips and listened to what was being broadcast in my head at the same time. That's when I realized that his jabbering matched the very words trapped inside my head. *Why, were my hearing aids on the same damn frequency as that order-taking system? But how, in the name of God, could that happen?*

And just as I flicked the plastic in my ears one last time, I heard all this hissing and cracking like a radio dial caught between stations. And this time, that Southern drawl bawled in a whispered fit, *'Sweet Jesus! What do you mean you lost the money for payroll? You were supposed to go to the bank with it, you feckin' moron . . .'*

My heart took off. I clutched my purse to my bosom and shot my eyes all around. But in the faces surrounding me, folks were oblivious. They were all caught up in this fast-food abyss – gorging themselves on milkshakes and greasy corn dogs – without a care in the world. That's when I knew I was alone in this.

Oh, why couldn't I be as deaf as the wall right now, I thought, as the voice of that man with the billboard-size *Jesus* belt buckle rattled my hearing aids again.

"Friendly folks of the Freeze and Frizz," he announced, this time for *all* to hear. "If I may have your attention . . . It seems that a large sum of money from the front office has been misplaced. Now, knowing how all our patrons are decent, law-abiding citizens, we're asking that if anyone knows the whereabouts this money, they kindly come forward right away. We'd be much obliged . . ."

I swallowed a brick of air.

Georgette shook her head. Her eyebrows dipped and her mouth merged into a pitiful pout. "Oh, this is just awful - just terrible, Marjery!"

At that very moment, images of my fat-vacuumed body reclining in a plush, new La-Z-Boy in front of a large screen HDTV started to fade like a window wet with rain.

"Oh, c'mon, Georgette. It'll turn up. They do a good business here. I reckon that whatever they've lost is a mere drop in the bucket." My secret was rooting in my throat as I clenched tighter to my purse. "Anyway, I'm stuffed. How about we get out of here and mosey along?"

I pushed away my grilled cheese sandwich and rose to my feet, waiting for Georgette to join me. But instead, she marched straight away from the table - armed with her Bible. She rushed behind the food counter, pushed aside the man with the *Jesus* belt buckle and grabbed the long, metal goose-neck microphone as if she were waging a holy crusade.

"Men and Women of the Lord . . . God's put it upon my humble heart to stand here before you and ask that we all take a moment and get down on our knees and pray." Georgette's nasal voice ricocheted so loud inside my hearing aids that my eyes were crisscrossing. "Let us all put our hands together and ask the Lord for His merciful intervention at this time of tribulation . . ."

Chairs started scraping and folks were getting down on the floor. I just stood there - frozen. In one hand, I was holding my purse smack up against my belly. And with the other, my palm moistened around the cool, metal handle of my walker.

Georgette shut her eyes. She lifted her Bible to the ceiling and with fierce conviction pleaded, "Dear Lord. We beseech you to use your awesome power *right now* and invoke a miracle . . ."

In the midst of Georgette's plea, folks started crawling around on all fours as if on a scavenger hunt. But being that I was the only soul – besides Georgette and the man with the *Jesus* belt buckle – still standing, I figured I could get lost in the shuffle and make my get-away. Through the front, plate-glass window of the Freeze and Frizz, I could see the sky turning a deep, angry shade of purple and curtains of rain coming down in a fit. When I took a step toward the door, the ground beneath my orthopaedic shoes trembled and a violent crack of thunder shuddered through me so that my body fell to the floor in a clumsy heap. As I tried to wrestle myself up off the linoleum, the man with the *Jesus* belt buckle put his hands around the long, metal, goose-neck of the microphone to move it closer to Georgette, so she could finish reciting her appeal.

But the storm hit. A burst of electric pink lightning split open the sky. It reached down and stabbed right into the Freeze and Frizz, until the man with the metallic and rhinestone *Jesus* belt buckle got zapped with a burst of energy. His body vibrated as his hands stayed glued to that long, metal goose-neck microphone. He couldn't seem to let it go, as his belt buckle started glowing. It lit up the whole room like neon. *Jesus! Jesus!* It blazed into the room.

Folks started screaming, and I started slithering away on my hands and knees toward the door – trampling over limp, oily French fries and half-eaten hamburgers – weaving my body beneath the tables and dragging along my purse with that sack of money. And just as I was inches from a get-away, I saw the word *Jesus* burst into flames. That man's belt buckle launched off his belt. It shot clear across the room like a fiery torch and landed on the linoleum just inches from where I was crouched on my hands and knees, panting like an over-heated prairie dog.

I couldn't believe my eyes. That yellow and red fireball flared up right in front of me like a Fourth of July sparkler that fizzles and fades. I felt a shock rip through my head and a deafening shriek pierce my eardrums. And as I thrust my hands over my ears, my purse went flying so that the sack of money stashed on top went sailing out across that slick, greasy floor.

The man finally let go of that goose-neck microphone and collapsed into Georgette's arms, and the sound in my head finally ceased. All I could hear was silence as billows of smoke rose off that belt buckle until the lights inside the Freeze and Frizz suddenly flicked back on.

"Jesus A. Christmas!" I hollered, as that word *Jesus* was still glowing like a hot, branding iron searing deep into the linoleum. I looked around. Everyone was stone-faced. Silent. Their mouths unhinged, they were staring at me.

Without second thought, I reached for the sack of bills – wads of dollars were now spilling out like green stuffing.

"Why, lookie here," I announced. "Here it is! Here's the money!" I exclaimed, my quivering hands waving that brown, paper sack like a flag of surrender.

Eyes of joy turned upon me until folks started cheering, shooting their gazes up to heaven.

"Praise God! It's a miracle!" Georgette howled, firming her grasp around the man who was stripped of that *Jesus* belt buckle. He looked as stunned as I felt. His hair was standing up on end and his skin exuded this awesome, 14-karat glow.

Next thing I knew, Georgette was helping me back on two feet and ripping that sack away from my white fingertips.

"Good ole Matthew 13:13," she said, winning our tug-of-war. *"If they would just turn to me, says God, I would heal them* – and He did. He answered our prayers, Marjery – don't you see?"

Georgette reached down and fearlessly put her fingers around that still-smoldering rhinestone *Jesus*. With one hand, she raised up my arm, and with the other, she held up that sack of money and the belt buckle. "Let's hear it for Marjery Pettigrew - a true disciple blessed by our Lord!"

The whole Freeze and Frizz became drenched with applause and teardrops trickled down from my eyes. The wetness of them all sizzled and steamed when they dropped upon that word *Jesus* still emblazoned in the linoleum at my feet, marking the spot like holy ground.

KATHLEEN GERARD'S FICTION WAS AWARDED THE *PERILLO PRIZE FOR ITALIAN AMERICAN WRITING* (2007) AND WAS NOMINATED FOR *BEST NEW AMERICAN VOICES* (2003), A NATIONAL PRIZE IN LITERATURE. HER FICTION AND NONFICTION HAVE APPEARED IN VARIOUS LITERARY JOURNALS AND ANTHOLOGIES THROUGHOUT THE USA AND CANADA, AND SEVERAL OF HER ESSAYS HAVE BEEN BROADCAST ON NPR (NATIONAL PUBLIC RADIO, USA).

Greetings From The Abyss

by Tyler Bumpus

Behold the child:

He lumbers through the garden center of Flintmann's Department Store with one garish potted plant in each hand, carrying them to the customers' glittering red Tahoe parked by the curb. His work shirt sticks moistly to his back. The middle-aged couple chirp and grin and thank him for his help. He nods to them, smirking. His mouth a deep, empty incision. Dribble and brine upon his lips. The Tahoe rumbles away, becoming a single point of crimson light bleeding upon the heat-distorted landscape.

The child lights a cigarette, mops his brow with a forearm, sweating under a phosphoric noon sun. He hopes with all of his heart that their monstrous car will tumble over the Margate interchange and shatter upon the earth, catching fire. He imagines their hoarse cries, belching out from broiled lips, somehow fueling the flames that will blister their flesh and their leather upholstery into chalky black residue.

"Hotter'n hell," his co-worker Barry says to no one in particular from beneath the canopy of the garden center.

"I know, right?" the child says, surveying the shopping complex. "Oughta put this on a postcard, instead a the fuckin beach. Strip malls and highways and assholes sweating to death. This is Florida."

Barry snorts. "Yer a chipper one."

"Nah." He waves him off and tosses his cigarette, extinguishing it beneath his shoe. "It's just this goddamn heat."

The child's name is Lawrence. He dislikes the name because he discovered on the internet that its meaning is "man from Laurentum," a dead city in Italy. He sees no benefit in being named after something dead and forgotten. He has come to wonder if a great deal of the world isn't just as vacuous. A brazen and oblivious parody of itself. Glitz concealing all of life's shallowest cavities.

Lawrence leaves the store at 4:30 p.m. to go to his second job at a call center in Margate. Traffic on the interstate is bumper to bumper. A family in a blue minivan from Miami has been sideswiped by an 18-wheeler just before the Cypress Creek Canal on their way to the Walt Disney World Resort. Travelers ride their brakes to catch a glimpse of the rescue crew removing the dead family from their serrated cocoon. Lawrence himself cranes his neck as a small dangling body in a Mickey Mouse shirt is lifted from the back seat of the van.

He is late for work.

For eight hours, he is at the receiving end of consumer frustration: pro-rated bills, deceptive pay plans, faulty equipment, unwanted cell phone features, jealous husbands wanting their wives' phone records, cuckolded wives wanting their husbands' phone lines cancelled, and privileged fifteen year olds in desperate need of Bluetooth headsets. He trembles with quiet rage and imagines cutting their heads off with an electric knife. The kind his father would use to carve the Thanksgiving turkey. Flesh frayed and fibrous. Lawrence shakes his head, draws a deep breath and sort of chokes when it occurs to him. In a well-ventilated building, he can't blame such thoughts on the heat.

In the dead of night, when he arrives back at the HUD house that he and his girlfriend Candice lease for eight hundred dollars a month (plus utilities), she is still awake. She tells him that she is pregnant. Lawrence doesn't say a word. Doesn't even blink. He clears his throat noisily, pulls his button-up shirt up and over his blonde head, dropping it to the shabby carpet floor, and drifts into the bedroom. Emptying drawers of clothing into a duffle bag and a small suitcase.

"What're you doing?" Candice says.

"What's it look like?" Lawrence mutters and grabs the luggage, stepping back into the living room. "It's not mine."

"Whattaya mean 'not yers'? The hell kinda way's that to talk to a person?"

He shrugs. "Way to talk to a whore."

Her eyes become glassy and red but there is a guilty restraint to her response: "Why'd you say that?"

"We haven't fucked in half a year."

"Who's fault's that?"

He opens the front door.

"No! I'm sorry!" she says. "I'm sorry. I didn't mean that. I'm scared. Okay? Really goddamn scared."

"Right." He nods. "Then why don'tcha go get the father from whatever bar you found him in and ask <u>him</u> for a goddamn handout."

"Fuck you!" She erupts. "Fuck <u>you</u> faggot! If you could get it up—"

Lawrence shuts the door quietly behind him and crosses the brittle brown lawn, quivering in the humid night. Regaining composure, he empties his heart and his mind onto the dead grass behind him before climbing into his '95 Grand Am.

A quiet settles over the neighborhood like a veil, each craggy little house a separate headstone marking the empty fate of its occupants. Various curtained front windows glowing baby blue in the outer dark from TV-light. Their epitaphs.

"This is Florida," he says under his breath and starts the engine.

    #

The next afternoon, about one hundred miles north at a desolate exit off of Interstate 95, Lawrence hesitates as he passes a black man resting comfortably on the side of the road by the smoldering remains of a motorbike. Seeing that there isn't another soul for miles, he groans at his reluctant conscience, pulls his car onto the shoulder and waits for the man to approach the passenger side window. He rotates his shoulder weakly, smarting from a night spent on a flimsy Super 8 mattress.

"Hell, c'mon!" Lawrence shouts out the window, craning his head to see him, "Whaddya think I stopped for?"

Still stretched out contentedly on the hot pavement like someone lounging on the beach, the black man shifts his gaze toward the car and stays that way for some thirty languid seconds before grinning wide and brandishing a staggering collection of moon-white denticles. He lifts himself easily from the asphalt and as he rises, unfolding to a full seven feet and change, Lawrence is taken aback and squints hard through the midday sun to get a better look at him.

The man strides toward the automobile along the worn

and wasted highway with the languor of a nobleman strolling the lavish excesses of some lost kingdom. Not a concern, not a care—only a quiet and curious mirth. Squinting through the sunshine, Lawrence fears, for a moment, that the man is naked like some ancient tribesman of Sudan. Even sees a spear gripped firmly in one hand. Upon approach, the spear reveals itself to be a broken tree branch. The man twirls it skillfully between his fingers. It is now discernable where flesh ends and clothing begins. He is dressed in parched black leather over his bare chest. Leather pants squeaking dryly in the sun as he steps, tapping out a gravelly rhythm with steel trimmed boots.

"Hell! Take yer time, man. Shit." Lawrence follows him with his eyes as he taps to a stop at the front passenger side of the car, declining to stoop down to meet his gaze through the window. "Gotta helluva fire going. What happened?"

"Bike died," he hears the man thunder in a deep, articulate bass over the roof.

"You don't say?" Lawrence scoffs, eyeing the flames cautiously. "Hell. Yer lucky I came by when I did."

"That so?" The man's crotch remains framed in the passenger window.

"Yeah, that's so. You anxious to camp out on the highway?"

There was a deep, cavernous silence.

"Are you offering a ride?"

Lawrence bristles a little at the subtle apathy of this ungrateful negro. "Shit," he says and shakes his head, spits out the driver's side window. "Yeah, sure. For a ways. Where you live?"

"I have many residences."

"'Many residences.'" Lawrence scoffs again. "Which one you lookin to go to? Shit, ifya wanna stay out here, it don't matter much to me. Just tryin to be a good Samaritan."

The tree branch kicks up a cloud of dirt as it smacks the ground. The passenger side door opens and the man's massive dark frame folds absurdly but skillfully onto the seat beside Lawrence. When he is settled, he turns a piercing yellow-eyed gaze upon him.

"I suppose I'll just ride with you a ways," the man says.

"Is that right?"

The great man's mouth spreads into a vast simian grin.

"Look, I'm headin to Daytona. Up the coast," says Lawrence.

"Sounds like a start."

Lawrence looks the cyclopean man over, avoiding eye contact. He shrugs, puts the car into gear and takes off up Interstate 95.

#

Silence reigns in the cabin of the car as the sun slinks below the western horizon. Lawrence grips the steering wheel uneasily, unable to deny the fact that since picking the behemoth up from the roadside an hour ago, an uncanny feeling has washed over him. A great rise in barometric pressure, a shift of electromagnetic fields.

"So, lemme ask you," Lawrence says, "what're you doin out here, anyway?"

"I have been called."

"You been called?"

"I have been called, Lawrence. I have decided to answer that call."

Lawrence falters and the automobile swerves.

"How you know my name?"

A smirk. "Your nametag. Lawrence."

Lawrence peers down at the Flintmann's Department Store_nametag nestled in the cupholder. "Right. Well, I'm not workin right now and you and me aren't really on first name basis, if it's all the same to you."

"It is all the same to me," says the man. "You are upset. Why are you upset, little man?"

"Not upset."

"Before you stopped at the side of the road, you were vacillating."

"Man, I was just tryin to make heads or tails of what I was seeing."

"Why did you hesitate, Lawrence? You almost continued down the highway. Was it because of the color of my skin?"

"Shit! Don't even start with the NAACP shit. I'll kick you to the curb right now. My dad fought beside guys like you.

Color's got nothing to do with anything."

"'Guys like me.'"

"Right. You know what I'm sayin."

"Do you mean <u>niggers</u>, little man?"

"Hell, I didn't say that," Lawrence says, fidgeting.

"Your father fought in Viet Nam?"

"That's right."

"Marvelous! And did your grandfather shoot japs? Did your great-grandfather slice up some injuns at Wounded Knee?"

Lawrence's knuckles whiten with pressure against the steering wheel. "What's that supposed to mean?"

"Would you like me to cherish your father's memory because he didn't particularly mind joining niggers in the killing fields against less agreeable races?"

"No! I—Hell! Yer mincin words now—"

The man releases a deep happy laugh. "It's okay, Lawrence. I understand. I understand everything."

Lawrence glances at him, catching his great ivory grin and wild mustard-threaded eyes. His complexion is the darkest of any black man Lawrence has ever seen, like some rare obsidian born deep within the mountains of ancient Africa.

"What's <u>yer</u> name, anyhow?" he asks.

"Nat Turner," the man says sharply and grins.

Lawrence braves that horrid gaze. "Pretty funny."

"What is funny?"

"Nat Turner. One that led that slave revolt in Virginia way-back-when, killing whites."

"Is death a funny thing to you, Lawrence?"

Lawrence clears his throat uneasily. "What's yer <u>real</u> name?" he says.

"You may call me Thaddeus. Thaddeus Belia."

"Oh, I <u>may</u>, eh? The hell kinda name's that?"

"What kind of name is Lawrence Burroughs?"

Lawrence freezes and shoots Thaddeus an anxious glance before searching frantically across the front of the car, his eyes coming to rest on an old cell phone statement crumpled on the dash.

"I spose you just read my last name off that bill there."

"I could have."

He squints at the man before turning back to the road. "Burroughs is English. Back in the early seventeenth century, most Burroughs went to the colonies to escape persecution in England."

"That's fascinating, Lawrence. I see you are well versed in the finer points of your name's history." Thaddeus's gaze is still on him, as it has been since climbing in. He smiles, in constant amusement with the twilight world around him.

Lawrence grinds his teeth. "Yer makin fun a me." He spits the words out, unsure whether it's intended as a question or a statement. "Well, whattabout yer name?"

"Thaddeus Belia is a combination of sounds that bear little meaning save that which I assign."

"'That which I assign.'" The muscles in Lawrence's neck tighten and he studies the moonlit clouds against the black of the eastern sky. "Sound pretty smart there."

"What? For a nigger?"

Lawrence blinks at him and Thaddeus laughs wildly. A laugh of sulfur and ember and crackling flame. Like great stones colliding in a quarry or the cry of some prehistoric creature echoing across vast gulfs of time. All of a sudden, Lawrence is nauseous.

"So, what are you running from, little man?" Thaddeus says.

"What? Nothin. Why?"

"Your car is loaded with luggage. And, evidently, you've no clear destination."

"It's none of your business."

Thaddeus nods, smiling. "'The mass of men lead lives of quiet desperation.'"

Lawrence shoots a look at him. "Who said that?"

"A babe in the woods."

The two of them fall silent and the rattle of the engine presides. In those several empty minutes, Lawrence is thankful that he has neglected a tune-up. Anything to put some space between himself and the unfathomable man. Privately, he likens conversation with him to a dance he can't quite pick up. It conjures memories of line dancing in middle school gym class.

Trying clumsily, perhaps unwillingly, to dance the Electric Slide and the Boot Scoot'n Boogie. Something in his heart resistant to the very notion of taking part in practices arcane and, therefore, in his mind, aimless.

"Look, guy, I didn't mean to cut you off before," Lawrence says sheepishly. "It's just private stuff."

"Ah! Horrific things."

"No, not <u>horrific</u>. Just normal things. Everyday shitty things."

Thaddeus nods. "Horrific things."

Lawrence bites his lip, nods vaguely. "Routine. Wake up, go to work, come home, find out yer girlfriend's fuckin someone else. Move on. Watch TV, pay yer bills, get married, buy a sports utility vehicle. Have children. Go to Disney. Get old. Rinse and repeat. Eat, shit, fuck, die." His voice cracks. "Get to a point where you ask yerself what the fuck people are for."

"And what <u>are</u> people for?"

Lawrence stares at the giant for a moment, shakes his head. "Got me. Each other, I guess. We're sposed to endure, drive each other up the wall. Be part of a system, wait for it to get us to the moon or Mars so we can eat and shit and fuck and die on other planets. Spread out." He shrugs. "Hell, I dunno. It's all so goddamn ugly."

"You know what the most useless part of the human body is?" Thaddeus says, drumming his hand atop the dash in a random and childish manner. "The eyes. You cannot trust the eyes. Silly things—see only what they want to. You know what's second most useless? The ears. Then the tongue. And the nose. And the nerve endings beneath the skin. All easily deceived. Defective. They cannot even begin to tell you truth about this world."

"The truth?"

"It's not ugly, Lawrence. It's just coming down, little by little. Balancing."

"That's a pretty sour way of lookin at it."

"Not if you look at it the right way."

"And how's that?"

"Every thing on earth is precisely the same."

Lawrence considers this, eyebrows furrowed. "How so?" he says.

"Put it to flame and it turns to ash."

"Huh." Lawrence slackens his grip on the steering wheel, looks out the window to the shadows enveloping his car. A gloom complete and inflexible. He wonders at man's fear of the darkness. Is it the fear of wickedness? The fear of the unknown? Or a fear of the innate? The midnight blackness residing in each and all. Encoded in the very molecules. Base and carbon, neither quantified nor judged. In the dark— equality.

"I guess I'd never—" Lawrence murmurs, trailing off into silence.

#

It is after 11:00 p.m. when they pull into a BP Station on the outskirts of Daytona that lingers in the surrounding darkness like a inexplicable beacon of light and meaning. Five customers huddle in the bright interior of the convenience store like the parishioners of a garish chapel, doddering down aisles with feigned purpose. Eyes studying racks of beer and candy and condoms.

Lawrence gets out of the car and stretches his legs but Thaddeus Belia remains in his seat. Leaning down, he looks at Thaddeus through the driver's side door.

"So...where you lookin to get dropped off, man?"

"So isolated," Thaddeus says, eyes fixed on the convenient store. "Like the end of the world out here." He chuckles convulsively.

Lawrence blinks and yawns. "Seriously, man. You wanna ride further into Daytona? Or you wanna call someone here to pick you up?"

"Oh, no. This is perfect right here." The great black man turns to Lawrence grinning. "Right where I'm supposed to be."

Lawrence furrows his brows at him. "What're you sayin? This is where you were headed—this gas station?"

Thaddeus Belia doesn't answer.

"Look, I gotta take a piss."

"Indeed, Lawrence."

Lawrence pauses, clears his throat indelicately. "Could you get outta the car?"

"Of course, Lawrence," Thaddeus says, watching the convenient store window with rapt attention as he unfolds his body from the car. "Of course."

"Nothin personal. Just don't know you too—"

"Not a bit of it, not a bit." Thaddeus grins and waves him away, drifting past the gas pumps and further and further into the night, eyes glued to the building as he vanishes in the darkness. "See you inside."

"Right," Lawrence says and shakes his head, locks his doors and proceeds to the bathroom.

After putting twenty dollars worth of gas into the tank, Lawrence walks through the dingy metal doors of the convenient store to pay. A small line is gathered at the counter while a black woman at the register fumbles with a new reel of receipt tape. Lawrence sighs, gripping a sweaty wrinkled twenty in his palm.

He picks up a postcard from the rotating postcard rack. A charming image of a tropical sunset over cool crystalline waters, sable palms drooping lazily toward soft golden sands. It reads: Greetings from the Sunshine State!

The man in line behind Lawrence groans through his teeth. "That's right. Take yer time," he hisses under his breath. "Nigger bitch."

The hairs on Lawrence's neck stand on end as he turns away from the picturesque image to see the man. Young, white, tattooed, lit cigarette gripped between his teeth. Clutching a twelve-pack of Coors.

"Fuck you lookin at?" the man snaps at Lawrence. "Faggot."

Lawrence turns back around, flushing with rage. He says nothing in return. The man is too big. He cannot take him.

"You can't smoke in here," the black woman at the register says, pausing until she has the tattooed man's attention. "Sir? You can't smoke in here."

"Not wastin it. If you'd hurry the fuck up, I could buy this and get out," he says.

"I'm going as fast as I can and there's no smoking in here."

"Fuckin bitch."

The woman smacks the counter. "Excuse me?"

"Ah, don't get all uppity, bitch."

"You can leave right now!"

"Fuck yerself."

A terrible sensation overcomes Lawrence while these two trade hostilities, something he cannot explain. More than disgust or shame or aggravation. Something internal. Like hot insects beneath his flesh. A rage dormant and ancient. Inherent in the veins of creatures meek and corralled—helpless to their natural vulnerabilities to the world. Lawrence begins fidgeting, squirming beneath his moist flesh. Something volcanic within him seethes. Look: he trembles.

"Who summoned me from the pits?" The voice cuts through all of the commotion of the convenience store. The room falls into an awkward silence. A few heads turn toward the front door of the shop and avert their eyes immediately, like antelope unsettled by the presence of a leopard. "Who summoned me from the pits?!" Lawrence freezes because he recognizes the deep tenor of the voice and turns to look at the front door.

Thaddeus Belia stands in the doorway in his dusty leathers, yellow eyes blazing, and sets a sloshing bucket on the floor. "Who summoned me from the pits?!" he shouts again, his face twisted in a distant and delighted rage. The employee and the customers stiffen, trying to continue on with business as usual.

"Fifteen dollars," she tells the customer in front of her. The woman trembles as she pays the cashier.

"Who summoned me from the pits?!"

A flash of movement from the entranceway. Lawrence turns, frozen in awe, to see Thaddeus spring forth and clutch the tattooed man by the neck, sinking his great gleaming teeth into the meat of his shoulder. The man tries to scream but has no voice. He burbles like an infant. A crimson stream springs up to Thaddeus's mouth like oil from the earth and he spits a hunk of sinewy tissue onto the floor, taking the man by the throat with both hands. The man jitters and flails but Thaddeus drags him to an end aisle stacked with Pringles cans and hammers his head against the corner of the steel support frame until the top left of his skull bursts and empties it's red dregs upon the shelving.

One person gives half of a cry and a few others gasp and waffle about. Thaddeus lets the man slink, twitching, to the floor and turns his yellow gaze upon the crowd. Somebody whimpers and Thaddeus steps calmly over the body on the floor, takes a middle-aged woman with a Biketoberfest t-shirt gently by the shoulder, pushes her slowly to the ground and stomps her squirming head until it comes apart in wet shaly slabs.

The cashier and a heavy set man with thick glasses retreat to the back of the store by the refrigerated beer cases, hands clutching their mouths. Lawrence falls back against a food shelf and releases an avalanche of Nestle's Crunch to the linoleum floor. The postcard slips from his grip.

"Chin up, now!" Thaddeus says as he bludgeons an older man in khaki shorts, boat shoes dangling from milky, hairless legs. "This is just a taste! A postcard from me to you! 'Greetings from the Abyss!'" The behemoth heaves the man onto the counter and pushes his head through the plate glass of the scratch-off ticket case. The man suffocates, throat punctured, gurgling spit and blood and mucus upon rolls of enticing and vibrant game tickets.

Thaddeus whips around, paces to the door, grabs the bucket and begins dousing the store with gasoline. The fluid glitters golden in the pale fluorescent light. The cashier cries out from the back and Thaddeus drops the bucket and strides back towards her, panting excitedly through his great nose.

When Lawrence hears the shrill and mammalian cries from back by the beer cases, he scrambles toward the door, slipping in a pool of gasoline and falling on his face. By the time he regains his footing, the store has caught fire. He tries to push his way through the automatic doors, but they are unresponsive.

He is pounding the glass with quivering fists when he is seized from behind and finds himself face to face with Thaddeus Belia. His body naked and shimmering in the firelight. In his eyes, Lawrence witnesses an almost magmatic gleam.

"It's not ugly, little man. It's just balancing out," Thaddeus says, great teeth gleaming like that of a tiger.

The smell of burning gasoline stings Lawrence's nostrils. "Please!" He wriggles in Thaddeus's grip.

"But this is your routine ending," Thaddeus whispers. "This is all things being equal. Know what I see when I look at you? At this town? At everyone?"

Lawrence shrinks away, trembling.

The room quakes, flames lick the ceiling. Thaddeus Belia pulls Lawrence closer, a grip like hot steel. "Ash, little man! Soot! Some things burn quicker than others but, Lord, they all burn!" He laughs horribly.

Lawrence turns away, shuts his eyes. "What are you?" he whimpers.

"Candor, brother! Pure and unprejudiced! Not black, not white! I have no name!"

Thaddeus takes him into a delighted, crushing embrace and plants his blood-stained lips upon Lawrence's. Lawrence shrieks, struck by a sensation that his body and mind and heart are alight and lay bare before a purblind world.

He thrusts backward through the glass door and flails through a hail of twinkling glass shards and away from the burning store, stumbling to a halt at the street. He watches for a long time, entranced by the speed and fury with which the fire works through the partitions and reduces it to carbon skeletal framework. Somewhere distant a fire engine screams in his direction, much too late to alter the inexorable.

Flames swallow the building in one mass immolation, burning away the walls between civilization and the natural world. Consuming man and dwelling alike—all things reduced to a form base and black and blended. Lawrence squints in the dark and catches an amorphous movement at the center of that blackened rubble. Thaddeus Belia is still there, somehow untouched. He grins horribly and lays his great black body prostrate upon a bed of cinder, bathing in the ebon residue. Hot powdery concoction of what had once been man or structure, now indistinguishable. Forever equal. He laughs wildly, yellow eyes blazing, making angels in the ash. He says that the world is balancing, balancing. All things becoming harmonious. He says that he is home.

BORN AND RAISED IN THE SUBURBS OF ORLANDO, FL, WHERE HE TAUGHT HIMSELF TO WRITE, READING THE LIKES OF FLANNERY O'CONNOR, MARK TWAIN, CORMAC MCCARTHY AND KURT VONNEGUT JR. IS A SOLEMN BELIEVER THAT THE VERY BEST AND MOST EARNEST

METHOD TO LEARN WRITING IS TO AVOID CREATIVE
WRITING COURSES AT ALL COSTS AND TO ATTEND THE
LOCAL LIBRARY. IS ONE OF TEN CHILDREN.

CONTACT INFO:

EMAIL: TBUMPUS@GMAIL.COM

THE DREAM MACHINE
BY JUSTIN C GORDON

Successful people have successful thoughts. That's from page one of The Dream Machine rep's handbook. In the hall mirror, I repeat this mantra as I fasten my silver cufflinks. These were my prize for selling the most Dream Machines last October. Forget it's May; they're real silver. They have enough value to pawn.

I gather the Dream Machine's large box and move to the kitchen. My wife, Debbie, reads the want ads while our ten-year-old son, Jimmy, chomps cereal. I lift my lunch bag off the table. It feels light. "P.B.N.J?"

"There isn't anymore lunchmeat." Debbie says and looks away. In most households this means inconvenience, but for us it's an economic barometer.

"Peanut butter 'n' jelly is great, Mom." Jimmy wraps his arms around us. He's become our glue. "I know you're gonna sell lots of Dream Machines today, Dad."

After Jimmy runs off to school, Debbie's pretty "mom" face fractures into deep worry lines. "Bill, we're going to lose everything."

"I'll break this streak, like before." I say to my shoes.

From a box underneath the calendar Debbie picks up a pile of collection notices and says, "That stupid vacuum cleaner is going to destroy us!"

I plead, "Honey, it's a Dream Machine: *it guarantees success.*"

Debbie pitches the mail at me then runs out of the room crying. Unpaid bills smack and slide off me. Some land into the sink where scraped clean jars of P.B.N.J. sit. An empty bread bag hangs out of the trashcan. My successful thoughts stumble.

At work, the room is filled with two-dozen salespeople trying to sound casual while reciting a sales pitch script into phones. Mornings are for cold calls, which are just any number in the white pages my pencil tip falls on. Everyone's goal is to set up afternoon appointments and demonstrate the Dream Machine.

My boss calls himself Dick Diamond. He has a speck of glass on a gold front tooth bought by selling so many Dream Machines. Near lunchtime, Dick Diamond carries in a bucket of chicken drowned in barbeque sauce and signals for silence.

"Everyone stay seated." Dick asks. "Is anyone hungry today?"

My mouth drools. I look at my squished PBNJ in a sandwich bag. I stare at the bucket in his hand longingly. Dick tells me to stand up. He walks around to all of the other salespeople, offers them some chicken, and then asks loudly, "Does anyone know what kind of animal a salesman is?"

Someone behind me howls.

"Yes, a wolf! A salesman is a wolf on a hunt!" Dick finishes circling the room, reaches into the bucket, and pulls out a drumstick. "A wolf catches the hunt! A wolf bring home the hunt to the pack and no one goes hungry!" My boss points the drumstick at the sales chart on the wall, walks over to it, and taps the chicken against an empty row. Barbecue sauce is smeared by my name, "Bill, you're not selling, so you're not..."

Everyone glares at me with greasy lips because I'm holding up their cold calls and interrupting their hunt. I answer, "A wolf."

Dick turns away "And that makes you a goddamn possum."

My voice pleads, "I'll sell it."

"Sell it today or you're fired." He walks out of the room, "I don't need a possum."

The PBNJ feels so cold and so thick in my throat, I worry about choking on it.

I drive to the first address on my sales list and ring the doorbell. I think successful thoughts. I will sell this machine and when the door opens, I explain they've won a free shampooing of their house with The Dream Machine.

If the customer has a baby crawling on the carpet, I tailor the pitch. The Dream Machine stops assailants from preying on our families. I attach a paper filter to the Dream Machine and sample a small area of their carpet. The filter becomes swollen with black clumps of pollen, pet dander, and dust mites. I show them a large laminated photo of a magnified dust mite eating dead skin cells.

The customer always snatches their baby off the floor.

I ask if they have any stains they can't remove. They usually show me something red, like cranberry juice or spaghetti sauce on beige carpeting. I switch on the shampoo attachment; spray the area, and the Dream Machine takes action.

"Well look, where'd the stain go?" I ask.

They ask the price. This is where my dry spell begins: Two grand.

I live at the bottom of the Louisiana food chain. We work in casinos, oil refineries, or chemical factories and everyone lives from P.B.N.J. to P.B.N.J.

I am not a possum.

I vacuum their mattresses to show them the toxic molds they sleep in. They say no. I put on the extension wands and suck spider webs out of hard to reach places. They say no. I convert the vacuum into a leaf blower and clear refuse from their rain gutters. They say no. Dick Diamond phones to drop the price again and again. No. The price ends at nine hundred dollars, meaning both my Boss and I won't get anything but a star on the sales chart. No. Every month the sales channels offer a free trip for anyone that brings in fifteen stars. No.

I get in five "No's" before dusk.

My cold calls have sent me onto the other side of Lake Pontchartrain. This is middle of nowhere swamps. I finally find a gas station and it has a bar in the back. A pasta strainer is fastened above the entrance. The air stinks of fish and factory belch. I claw coins from dark places in my car for a beer. It's sick that a beer costs less then a sandwich.

The bar is busy with an after-work crowd from the refineries. It's coon-ass-ville: warped wooden floors, frayed seats, an alligator head near a crucifix, and no free snacks on the bar. No one talks. Their thoughts are like mine; drink to ignore the panic that comes from creditor calls and repo threats. There's a stool at the far end, beside an old man with a face like an albino raisin. He balances himself between a cane and the lip of the counter.

A draft is in my budget. I use my phone quickly, uncertain when they'll cut service off for nonpayment. Three calls just ring and one hangs up twice.

"You look like you just lost your best friend in the whole world." The old man props his hands and chin on his cane's handle.

"If you call a paycheck a best friend." I say and put away my phone.

"Then what are you doing out here in these swamps?" He smiles. "Let me guess, either your car broke down or you're a door-to-door dancer?"

I take a sip of my flat draft and say, "The second one."

He drums his lips with a finger thoughtfully for a minute and then asks, "Do you know why there's a colander above the door out there?"

"No clue."

"It's for the Cajun werewolf; Loup-garous." He says. "The Loup-garous has to count all the colander's holes before it can enter."

"You're joking?"

He shakes his head, "Ask anyone here."

"What happens when the thing finishes counting?"

"Usually, by then the sun's up and they're human again. It's easier to shoot them when they're human." He shrugs, "Otherwise throw a frog at them."

"Why a frog?"

"Frogs make them explode for some reason."

I laugh in disbelief, "I'll remember that."

"So unless you're selling colanders, I don't think you'd have a good audience here."

I notice his clothes are casual expensive and ask, "So did you break down or are you a salesman?"

"Not door-to-door. I dabble with old things for auctions." He smiles slyly, "There's lots of old things in these swamps and oil companies help me get them."

He explains that by profession, he's an archeologist. Oil companies can't drill anywhere without excavating first. It's a federal law they haven't been able to get rid of. His business squares off so many feet, hires students to dig up artifacts, and then he assess if the location has a significant historical value. This determines if the oil companies can drill there.

"You ever stop them from digging anywhere?"

His face changes so fast I feel like I slapped him. The cane touches his right foot. "Once, but the findings didn't suggest it was a good place to drill." He relaxes. "I mean, for historical reasons of course."

I ask, "Where do you sell artifacts?"

"There's no money in museum collections. Better to go with private collectors." He offers his hand, "My name is Milton. Milton Throckmorton."

We shake, "Bill Maxwell, Dream Machine representative."

"That sounds wonderful. What is it?"

I'm careful not to give him a pitch. When salesmen meet, they know the pitch is bullshit. I talk about technical details and what I've seen the product do. The more calmly I speak, the more excited Milton becomes.

"I have a problem." He says. "I have a rather big dog, an Irish Wolfhound. Ever see one? Loves to hunt, but brings his catch inside. Ruins the carpet."

"Is this your Loup-garous?" I ask. There are too many wolf references today.

"Wolfhounds hunt wolves." He shrugs. "Bring a frog if you want. I'm old and need a large dog for security. Your machine might be a solution to cleaning up after my dog. Show me it in action. Maybe you can go home without it."

Successful thoughts.

Outside, it's dark. Milton starts his red MGB. "Just follow me in your car."

I get into my beat-up Rabbit. Milton floors it. I chase. The winding road seems to leads further into swampland forever, but then a train of ground lights begins to appear. These end at a large security gate and we slow to a stop. Out his window Milton waves a remote. The massive iron door opens to a painfully manicured lawn and a giant plantation house. The front porch has columns too wide to hug.

Scarlet O'Hara, eat your heart out.

As I get The Dream Machine out of my trunk, Milton excitedly talks about his houses' renovation project, how the details matter more then the whole. "Like this stain in my study; nutria blood. Ruins the feeling of the whole house."

The house is a museum. Milton passionately points out ancient treasures: Spanish coins, pirate's swords, a Capuchin Friar's bible, and Arcadian dueling pistols. "These are just a few things I've acquired. I also have warehouses."

Milton leads me into a study with double doors to a patio. Thick books fill the shelves. On the wall is our state's topical map dotted with thumbtacks for digs and finds. Below it is a slanted top desk with a laptop displaying a Japanese auction website. Across the room, a black ceramic mug with two handles sits on an end table beside a leather sofa. On the white carpet is a dark red football-sized stain.

"This is called a tyg. It's a seventeenth century beer mug." Milton picks up the mug, "The second handle is for passing it on." He hands it to me and then stabs the stain with his cane. "I've made my cleaning woman cry over this damn spot. Skip the song and dance, show me what you can do, and I'll get us some wine."

I gently place the tyg back on the end table. I set up The Dream Machine; plug in the cable, attach the shampoo piece, pour the cleaner, and saturate the spot. The machine creeps over the shiny reflective bubbles and pulls on the edges of the stain. It's possible the stain is set, that the cards are against me, but I have a chance. I have the Dream Machine.

The stain goes from red to pink, slowly lifting. I give it another shampoo treatment and pay attention to the details like he said.

Nutria is the rabbit's ugly cousin. They have big buckteeth, grow to about knee high, and have long rat-tails. Poor people train them to charge salesmen.

The stain is gone.

I'm dizzy. I'm loopy. I've won. I'll really close this deal. I run the Dream Machine over the rest of the room and under the couch. There is an ugly clicking sound from something the silver-plated motor has sucked in.

I turn off the machine; drop to my knees, and pop open the motor. Inside is a hard white piece no larger then a fingertip and I'm terrified I've destroyed a dinosaur bone.

"What do you have there?" Milton holds two wine glasses.

"The machine sucked this in."

"Take this." He exchanges a glass for my find.

Milton turns it over carefully. "Do you know what this is?"

Sweat dots my upper lip as I say, "Nutria tooth?"

"Why yes." He pockets the damn thing and offers a toast.

We clink glasses. I watch Milton drain his glass in one swallow. I copy him. The wine is smooth. Milton moves to his desk, sits down, leans to the side, and disappears from view. I hear a lock spin and a metal door open. Milton sits back up and asks for the price.

I lower my eyes and answer.

"I see." He says and touches his fingertips together, "You do take cash?"

I can't hide my smile and feel dizzy. The room blurs. My legs are numb. I try to steady myself with the Dream Machine's handle.

Milton stands. "Bill, are you okay?"

"No." I fall on my back.

Milton opens the double doors to a dark patio. "Good."

I am paralyzed. Indigo spots swim before my eyes almost covering a full moon over the backyard. I go blind and hear Milton hobble away until his footsteps are lost in crickets and cicadas songs.

I blew the sale.

The insects become silent. A panting starts. It gets closer and louder. The room feels hotter. An incredible pressure builds against my skull with each pant, like my brain will squirt out my nose.

My eyes open slowly and focus on a large grey dog sniffing The Dream Machine. Green snot trails from its nose over the chrome finish. Large doesn't define the animal's size; hulking comes closer. It has shaggy matted hair and rows of sharp yellow teeth with strings of drool.

Milton's dog notices me. It growls like a revving diesel truck.

I am a possum. Possums play dead and get left alone. This beast wants to hunt. It wants to chase something that's alive. If I flinch it will pounce and rip open my throat. If I blink I will never see my beautiful wife or child again.

A big furry front paw rises and lands next to my face. It sinks deeply into the carpet and black nails graze my nose. I stare past it ignoring how my dry eyes feel like cigarette cherries are being slowly ground down into them. Milton's Dog steps awkwardly over me. One of its back legs hops to keep balance.

Its' breath stinks of dead foul things. My stomach turns sour. I'm going to puke. I feel it rising up my throat when a cold wet nose presses against the middle of my neck, shoving down on my vertebrae. This keeps the puke down. Then, Milton's dog starts sniffing my armpits. I almost shudder because it tickles.

I am a possum.

It sits back and howls. The windows seem ready to shatter.

I am a possum.

Milton's dog whines disappointed, steps over me, and pisses on my chest.

I am a marked possum fire hydrant.

It slowly pads out the patio doors.

There is no such thing as Loup-garous.

The full moon turns the dog's gray hair silver before it struts into the night. I must get out. Forget the machine. If Milton wants it that badly, he can keep it. Dick Diamond can come pick it up and get eaten. I'll never go door-to-door again.

Slowly I stand and stare out the open back doors. There's nothing but the moon. I step to the left, trip on the Dream Machine's cable, and crash into the end table. The tyg slides over the edge. Suddenly, there is so much damn noise.

Milton's dog bolts in. My leg is in its mouth. Its teeth dig down. Its head shakes, trying to rip my ankle off. I'm reaching for anything to stop it. The Dream Machine rises up and I smash it down on that damn dog's head. I smash again and again. The gray hair turns red. My ankle is ready to snap like a toothpick, but The Dream Machine stops assailants from preying on our families.

Milton's dog collapses.

A yellow mist rises from its fur with a rotten-egg stench. Smoke chugs out of the beast's mouth and I get the hell away. The dog deflates. Its hair singes like Fourth of July sparklers. My eyes sting so I wave madly at the smoke. It parts and I can see the side of the dog's broken face with a human eye. I swear to God it sees me, winks, but then the awful yellow smoke covers it up.

When the smoke finally clears, there's a really bad stain on the carpet.

I'm feverish. My leg looks like ground meat with yellow puss. I'm going to puke and I don't know why it matters, but I don't want to throw up on any of the museum stuff. I don't know why I'm not sprinting out of the house. I barely make it to a wastebasket behind the desk before everything inside me rips out of my mouth. I puke and puke and puke.

I've let my family down.

With what remains of my suit, I wipe up tears and snot strings. I hate successful people with successful thoughts. I probably have rabies. I check on my leg. I have no insurance.

There is no wound.

I sit there, staring at my ripped pants and studying my intact leg. I piece together a story. I tripped and hit my head on the end table. The dog came to eat me, Milton got in the way, and I used the Dream Machine to kill them both.

There is no such thing as a loup-garous, so the words 'murderer' and 'self-defense' jockey for first place.

Then I see something behind the desk; an open safe with enough money for five machines. The house is empty. The MGB is parked outside. The Dream Machine erases the evidence that anyone was ever here tonight.

No more P.B.N.J. ever again.

I've watched enough movies to know I have to keep quiet.

The day after Milton's dog, I call in sick on Dick Diamond's answering machine. I seal stacks of hundred dollar bills in plastic wrap. I tuck them under the attic's insulation, because sometimes it floods here. I take a full wallet to the casinos. I buy lots of chips, sit at a table and lose. If I win, I tip it to the staff. After an hour I cash out into twenty-dollar bills. No one at the supermarket inspects the serial numbers on a twenty.

I buy my display model and when my boss asks for the paper work, I tell him I sold it to a crack house. Dick Diamond loves selling to dealers because they pay cash and there's no sales tax. He slaps me on the back, calls me a wolf and puts a silver star on the sales chart.

I read the news every day. There's no mention of a Throckmorton murder or obituary. Milton's Dream Machine doesn't have a scratch on it. I throw it off the Huey P. Long Bridge and watch the heavy vacuum sink out of sight.

Almost every day I sell a machine. It's a simple game of deciding whose family is going to eat tonight and nothing is going to make mine go without ever again. Price doesn't matter; there are financing plans. I am a wolf on the hunt and catch the sale. Stars go up on the board. The boss puts a bucket of barbeque chicken on my desk and tells me not to share it with anyone. The other salespeople turn away, hiding their hungry faces, and quickly dial cold calls.

I savor the new smoothness in Debbie's face.

On the calendar in the kitchen, I mark off paid bills and see symbols for the cycles of the moon. Today's date is marked with a white circle in a black outline. At the table, Debbie asks Jimmy about a girl at school. He blushes brightly. My stomach drops and I think they're in danger. Maybe, Milton's dog could follow me home.

Even though there is no such thing as a Loup-garous.

I say I have a late sales call. Debbie complains, but kisses me for luck.

At a cheap hotel two hours from home I nail eight strainers throughout the room. I sit on the bed in my underwear, sweating, no a/c, and hold a colander by both handles.

I must look like a complete idiot.

Counting holes is hard work. I keep losing my place and have to start over. Hours pass. Nothing happens. I get bored, turn on the television, and "Braveheart" is on. I love that movie, except the end. When it's over, the clock says four: same time I left Milton's house.

See, there is no such thing as a Loup-garous.

As I check out, the clerk bumps his Bloody Mary and it spills on the carpet. He complains that inheriting a chain of seedy hotels is depressing. They're all filthy and stained buildings he wants to convert to business class. If there were just something that could help, he'd buy it in a heartbeat.

I close a deal with a chain of hotels. I win the trip. It's an all-expenses-paid vacation for my family to Disney World. So what if it's really a sales meeting.

We arrive at the dense and sweaty Orlando Airport, then get whisked to the Mouse compound. Our room is in the Caribbean area, not posh, but still lovely. You know something good is happening when you can leave your shaving hairs in the bathroom sink and someone else cleans it.

The meeting is at Epcot. Debbie and Jimmy love it. They hit the rides. I get face time with the Dream Machine's Inventor and CEO, Roffe Grandholm. He's a buff Swedish immigrant that carries himself like a Viking God of Vacuums. "I owe my success to two things. The first is my nationality. Swedes insist on very neat orderly houses."

"Like IKEA?" I ask.

"Exactly; boxes that neatly fit into other boxes." Roffe Grandholm laugh sounds like thunder. He shakes my hand and inspects my new gold Dream Machine cufflinks. "The second is successful thoughts. I see you have them too."

I attribute these solely to his machine and feel dirty, like I just gave him a hand job. He smiles pleased.

At dinner that night, marketing pages me. They feel the hotel chain is a hot topic and want to use me as a success story. Arrangements have been made for a photo of me with the Inventor and a Dream Machine at The World Showcase Lagoon. There, eleven different countries are represented as restaurants around a 41-acre lake.

And all you have to do to be here is kill someone and his pet. While the photographer sets up, I try to convince myself the hotel chain got me here. It doesn't work. Floating on the big silver Epcot golf ball is that dog's human eye.

It finds me and winks.

The Illuminations light show starts. A recorded female announcer is pleased to present an international fantasy of music and light. The Floridian sky is filled with fireworks. From behind the marketing pack, Debbie and Jimmy wave at me. The Flight of the Bumblebee symphony, with its seizure sounds blasts over the water. Lights flare on and off at the different countries. Machine-made smoke from the surrounding shore crawls across the lagoon's surface and meets in the center. There, a giant metal ball lights up with the names of each country.

The photographer calls me over.

"Clear sky tonight." Roffe Grandholm says as someone uses a lint brush on him.

"Good for the fireworks." I wince as someone else puts hairspray on me.

"I wonder where the moon is?" Roffe Grandholm cranes his neck around. "It's supposed to be a full moon tonight. Maybe Disney doesn't own it yet."

"The full moon was two weeks ago. I saw it on my calendar."

"That was the new moon." he pulls out his white cuffs. His gold cufflinks show. "Most calendars mark both phases."

I'm beginning to sweat. I don't need to. There is no such thing as a...

"Say, cheese." Roffe Grandholm suggests.

I crack a smile and it feels like a nail shoves through one of my top teeth. I stand there, shaking the hand of Roffe Grandholm with a Dream Machine between us, and have a pain so intense my legs are buckling. I grab my face. Roffe Grandholm looks concerned. I reach between my lips. My eyetooth gashes my finger.

The photographer gets huffy having missed his shot and then goes white. He drops the camera. The lens cracks against the asphalt. Blood spills out of my mouth as more teeth push down. From behind the Epcot ball peeks a full moon.

Success will never be mine.

Debbie covers Jimmy's eyes. She can't scream. I cover my mouth with a furry hand. Someone pulls Roffe Grandholm away. People collide. Parents grab kids. Sandals stomp pink cotton candy. An old woman makes the sign of the cross.

My family is frozen on the sidelines.

I tell them it's only a phase. It will pass. As long as they chain me up once a month, make me count holes; we can still be a family.

My explanation comes out as a piercing roar that flattens the hairs on their heads.

Time is running out. They don't know about strainers. There are no frogs available. The only thing between my family and a monster is a Dream Machine.

It stops assailants from preying on your family.

Milton can't have them. I'm not going to be a tyg and pass this on. I grab The Dream Machine and leap with powerful hind legs at the water. The bumblebee music shrieks. I splash into the deep lagoon filled with hundreds of lighting fixtures on miles of rollercoaster tracks.

Milton's dog wants out. It hates water. It knows I can't swim.

I quickly tie the Dream Machine's cable to a light fixture on a track that a chain is pulling toward the center of the lagoon. I loop the slack many times around my hairy neck. Dogs need leashes. The cable tightens. I'm dragged away from the shore, a graceless water skier on a noose while the Dream Machine trails along behind.

Milton's dog struggles and breaks the surface howling. Behind me, The Dream Machine gets caught in a cross shaped piece of track. I'm yanked back underwater. The light fixture moves forward while the trapped Dream Machine pulls back. The cord between them closes tightly on my throat.

Milton's dog resists. The light fixture is jerked to a stop and shines a white shimmering circle on the lagoon's underside. A gold cufflink sinks to the bottom. The Dream Machine looks ready to give, that the cable will rip out, but I've seen it in action. Even as metal chains pull the light fixture forward, as the shimmering circle turns a red the color of barbeque chicken, as my successful thoughts converge, it holds.

JUSTIN C GORDON WAS AN AWFUL VACUUM CLEANING SALESMAN IN LOUISANNA. COULDN'T EVEN SELL ONE MACHINE IN THREE MONTHS. ALMOST STARVED TO DEATH. THANK GOD FOR THOSE PLACES THAT BUY PLASMA. HE HAS PUBLISHED FICTION IN OUT OF THE GUTTER MAGAZINE, SOUTHERNGOTHIC.ORG, AND THE AMERICAN LITERARY REVIEW. HIS NOVEL, "THE ELECTRIC PICKLE" WAS ACCEPTED BY THE TAOS SUMMER WRITING CONFERENCE, WORKSHOPPED UNDER JOHN DUFRESNE, AND IS CURRENTLY BEING REVISED TO DEATH. HE LIVES OUTSIDE AUSTIN, TX WITH HIS WIFE, TWO SONS, AND A VERY LARGE DOG .

ACKNOWLEDGEMENTS

PJM PUBLISHING WOULD LIKE TO THANK THE FOLLOWING FOR THEIR INVALUABLE ASSISTANCE IN MAKING THIS PROJECT POSSIBLE.

THE JUDGES

RACHEL SYMONDS BSC MSC University of Sheffield

STEPHEN WINDLE - Screenwriter and director of the short film 'Alone In The Company of Despair'.

PAUL CLARKE - Radio Script Writer

HUGO CARMICHAEL - Book Editor and Freelance Writer

GENERAL SUPPORT

JEFF CROOK - www.southerngothic.org

www.welcometothevelvet.com

darkanimaliterary.blogspot.com

AND A FINAL BIG THANK YOU TO ALL THOSE WHO TOOK THE TIME TO ENTER A SHORT STORY.

PJM PUBLISHING

WWW.PJMORLEDGE.COM

Lightning Source UK Ltd.
Milton Keynes UK
UKOW032220100613

212043UK00007B/951/P